B/T

OUT OF REACH

BY *V. M. JONES*

MARSHALL CAVENDISH

Marshall Cavendish Corporation
99 White Plains Road
Tarrytown, NY 10591
www.marshallcavendish.us/kids

This book is a work of fiction. Names, characters, places, and incidents are products of the author's imagination and are used fictitiously. Any resemblance to actual events or locales or persons, living or dead, is entirely coincidental.

Library of Congress Cataloging-in-Publication Data
Jones, V. M. (Victoria Mary), 1958-
[Juggling with mandarins]
Out of reach / by V.M. Jones. — 1st North American ed.
p. cm.
Summary: Pressured by his aggressively competitive father to play soccer, teenaged Pip McLeod secretly pursues a sport that he truly enjoys—indoor rock climbing.
ISBN-13: 978-0-7614-5514-1
[1. Fathers and sons—Fiction. 2. Competition (Psychology)—Fiction. 3. Indoor rock climbing—Fiction. 4. Self-realization—Fiction.] I. Title.
PZ7.J72758Ou 2008
[Fic]—dc22
2007049515

Book design by Symon Chow
Editor: Robin Benjamin
The publisher wishes to thank model Aram Nercessian and Bryan Natter, manager of Island Rock indoor climbing facility in Plainview, NY.

Printed in China
First Marshall Cavendish edition, 2008
Originally published in 2003 as *Juggling with Mandarins* by HarperCollins*Publishers (New Zealand) Limited*

10 9 8 7 6 5 4 3 2 1

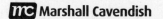

For my son Evan, with love

OUT OF REACH

THE MAN ON THE SIDELINE

He was there right from the beginning, of course . . . but at first, no one noticed him. Except me.

On one side of the field, with their backs to the watery sun, the parents: two straggling lines, one for each team, a discreet distance in between. The June sun was low, a typical New Zealand winter day, and I had to squint to see them.

And on the other side, a solitary figure in a faded green parka, already pacing up and down, impatient for the game to begin. Looking at his watch. Taking up his position, dead on the center line. Tension coming off him like steam, one hand raised stiffly to shield his eyes from the glare, like a cartoon cutout of a soldier on parade.

The other team's coach was reffing the first half.

I looked down, checking that my cleats were properly tied. They were secondhand, but the laces were new and extra-long, bought specially. Dad says the only way to do up soccer cleats is to wrap the laces right around underneath, and then tie them at the top. Not *on* top—then they get in the way when you kick the ball. "Always kick with the laces,

Son—the laces, or the side of the boot. Never a toe-hack. Toe-hacks are for Mites." Mites is the pre-competition baby grade. I'd played in it once—we all had, centuries ago. Now we laughed when we watched them, rushing around their tiny field after the ball in a harum-scarum bunch you could have covered with a postage stamp.

Patches of sticky mud showed through the grass, all squished and bruised-looking from the game before. The hair on my arms was sticking up. . . . They were covered in goose bumps, and these weird orange blotches.

At last, the whistle blew, and I felt my guts give that familiar lurch. The other team—the Rangers—kicked off—a show-off back-pass with the striker's heel; then a massive kick from their midfielder—my opposite number—came flying straight at me like a cannonball. Instinctively, I ducked and felt the whoosh of air as it missed me by millimeters.

I wheeled around and joined the stampede toward our goal, already sick at heart. I hadn't headed the ball; I'd ducked. Again. Without needing to look, I knew what the tall figure on the sideline would be doing. Jogging down the field, keeping pace with the players, his limp more noticeable because of the cold; eyes fixed on the ball, shaking his head and muttering: "Don't cringe *away* from the bloody ball— *head it*, dammit! What the hell's wrong with you?"

Still, there was time—lots of time. One little mistake early on wouldn't matter, because today I had a plan. Step One: do *one* basic thing—and do it well. Get into the game. Warm up; get involved. Then, when a couple of touches of the ball had got me in tune with the game . . . Step Two: get stuck in. *Really* stuck in.

Yeah! I made myself another promise: before this game was over, I'd do a header. A *real* header with my forehead, the way you're supposed to; the way I'd practiced a zillion times with Dad and Nick. *Smackeroo!* The ball would fly into the top corner of the net—and it wouldn't even hurt! The rest of the team would crowd around, punching me on the arm and giving me high-fives. Mentally I played the header: a run; a lunge; a leap, giving the ball that extra supercharge with my shoulders, that flick with the head to direct it straight into the goal . . .

"Philip!"

The bark from the sideline brought me back to Earth— literally, with a thump. Hopefully no one had noticed me jumping at nothing. If they had, they'd think I was psycho. I darted a glance at the boy marking me. He was chunky with sandy hair and freckles and a mean, scrunched-up face. He was staring at me with this mocking smile, like he knew something I didn't. "Dreaming of glory?" He cleared his throat and spat. The gob of mucus splatted onto the ground at my feet, like a squashed slug. "Dream on, retard."

The tussle at our goal was heating up. I heard a grunt and the thud of a foot connecting with the ball; saw the arm of Tom's multi-colored goalie jersey flash into the air and somehow connect with the ball and deflect it. A slim figure darted out from the mob of pushing, shoving players with the ball at its feet; dodged an attacker; looked up and saw me, jockeying for position in midfield with Squishface. "Pip!" it yelled, and drilled the ball down the line toward me.

I ducked out and intercepted it, hearing the crowd going crazy on one side, the lone voice on the other: "Your ball, Philip! Use it! Dig in! *Go all the way!*"

I turned on the outside of Squishface, returning his shoulder-barge with interest—*yes!*—focusing fiercely on the ball at my feet. Accelerated steadily, staying in control, keeping tabs on Squishface with an eye in the back of my head I never knew I had—dribbled on down the line, faster, faster, not letting the ball get away from me, ignoring the thunder of the other players bearing down on me and the rasp of Squishface's breath on the back of my neck. I knew I could hold him off. *I may not be tough, but I'm skinny and fast. Catch me if you can!* There was no one between me and the goal . . . no one except the goalie, legs and arms spread out and eyes wide, a look of panic on his face.

Here we go—this is it! Please, God, don't let me mess it up!

In the second it took for me to draw back my foot for the shot, a jumble of images flashed in front of me. The ball, scooting over the muddy grass, perfectly positioned for the kick. That same ball smacking into the corner of the net, rebounding, spinning in the mud like a top; me leaping after it, arms raised triumphantly, smashing it back into the net one more time for good measure. Dad's face. *Dad.*

Don't let me miss! I squeezed my eyes tight shut, and let fly. At the same instant, Squishface shot in from beside me in a crunching tackle; our legs tangled like cold spaghetti, and we hit the ground with a thump that rattled my brain and knocked the breath clean out of me. Dimly, I heard voices on one side yelling, "Great tackle! Brilliant defending!"

And from the other side: "Foul! Ref-er-reee! *Foul!* Tackle from behind! He kicked his legs right out from under him! *Penalty!*"

I didn't look. Instead, I picked myself stiffly off the ground and sat there trying to get my breath back, head spinning. Watching the ball roll harmlessly away into the longer grass beside the field, a good two meters off the goal. *I hadn't even connected with it.*

Then a pair of legs in muddy green socks was blocking my view. I knew those legs. Dizzily, I looked up, dazzled by the sun. A hand was reaching down and pulling me to my feet. Katie Wood. The girl next door—from way back. My best friend. Unofficially.

She scowled at me. "What kind of a shot was that, Dumbo? Honest, Pip, I wouldn't have thought even *you* could miss that one." Then, having made it quite clear to anyone listening that she was pissed off, adding quietly: "Hey—you okay?"

"Yeah, I guess. Great pass."

She shot me a grin and gave me a shove that nearly knocked me over again. "Well, do something with it next time!"

The goalie kicked the ball halfway down the field, and we were off again. I got a couple of touches in the next ten minutes, but I passed the ball quickly. *Before I could mess up.* I pushed the thought away before anyone could read it on my face.

The Rangers won a corner; Katie cleared it up to Mark, our left wing. Our coach says Mark's the only player in the league with two left feet, and five seconds later he'd scored with one of them—a beautiful curving shot the goalie couldn't even get a hand on. I risked a quick glance over to the sideline. One up. That was good. He'd be pleased.

But the equalizer came virtually from the kickoff—a classy little set play back and forth between the Rangers midfielders; then a lofted ball up to their striker who appeared from nowhere and kicked the ball past Tom, who wasn't even in his goal. The Rangers' supporters went crazy; heads down, we trudged back to our positions.

The voice rang out across the field like a trumpet. "*Offside!* Do you need glasses, Ref? That player was a mile offside!"

The Rangers coach had been lining himself up to blow the whistle for the kickoff. He shot an irritated glance over at the sideline and raised the whistle to his lips.

"Call yourself a referee? Or do you only see what you *want* to see?"

For a moment, it was as if everything froze. *Ignore him*, I prayed. *Blow the whistle—let's get on with the game. Then it will be over, and we can all go home.*

The coach turned to the man on the sideline, who was standing with his arms folded and a belligerent scowl on his face. "It wasn't offside," said the coach in a neutral voice. "The defender—the girl with the braids—was level with him when the ball came through. Now, can we please get on with the game?"

Yes, I echoed. *Can we please get on with the game?*

"That's the third offside you've missed. And the foul. And the handball off the corner."

For a long, long moment, the two men faced each other. One, whistle still poised, out of breath from keeping up with the play, his face beginning to tighten into real annoyance. The other, bulky shoulders bunched under the parka, head thrust forward like a bull about to charge.

Suddenly the ref smiled, and walked over to the sideline. He held out the whistle. "Here," he said pleasantly. "You do it."

"Huh?"

"Go on. You're the expert. *You* ref the match."

A muffled giggle rippled through the Rangers' players, who were standing in a muddy cluster watching to see what would happen next. I saw one of them nudge the guy next to him, and give him a thumbs-up.

"I—uh . . ."

The Rangers' coach had come right up to him now, still smiling and holding out the whistle. "Here you go. It's all yours."

The tall dark guy took a shuffling step back. His face, red with anger before, was even redder now. "I didn't mean . . . I'm not saying I . . ."

"Well, what are you saying? According to you, I'm not qualified to ref this match. But someone has to do it. So be my guest."

There was another long silence, as if time had stopped. On the opposite side of the field the parents were watching, mesmerized. Somewhere far away a bird called, the sound carrying with startling purity through the clear air: *Oodle-aardle-doodle-dardle.* Someone sniggered.

At last: "You carry on."

"Sure? Now are you *quite* sure? Because the next comment from you, mate, and I'm walking off this field and you're on. Understood?"

Another hard look, and the coach jogged backward onto the field. Then at last he turned back to us, standing watching, mouths open. "Come on, kids," he said. "We're here to play soccer. Let's do it."

Somehow, we'd all huddled together—though I couldn't remember moving. I felt sick.

Squishface grinned and whispered loudly, "Random, man! Is that your coach?"

"Nah," muttered Katie, looking away. "Our coach is over there—the blond guy on the left."

"Who's he, then?" Squishface asked, taking up his position alongside me. He had the same look of greedy curiosity on his face some people have when they drive past car accidents. "Huh, retard? *Who?*"

I looked down. One of my laces was coming undone. "I dunno. Just . . . some guy," I mumbled, crouching to fix it.

"What a loser," said Squishface flatly.

DAD

I never did get that header. We won—Colts three, Rangers two. But by then, I was way past caring.

Not Dad, though. He's never past caring.

He was in fine form as he stripped off his green parka and threw it in the back next to my bag. Hot from running, cold inside, I clambered up into the passenger seat of our ancient, battered four-wheel drive and sat there, staring out the window.

Tom walked past with his parents and kid brother, the Player of the Day trophy gleaming in his hand. He didn't see me.

Katie and her mum were heading for their blue station wagon. Katie was chattering away, as usual. I lifted up one hand to wave, but she was too busy talking to notice.

The driver's door opened and the truck gave a lurch, and suddenly it was full of Dad. Dad's like that—he seems to take up all the available space, though he's not fat or anything. He put the key into the ignition, ran his hands through his wiry black hair, and gave the steering wheel a resounding slap. "Well, Son, three-two, against the odds. How about that? Not a great win, but a *win*; and that's all that counts." He turned the key; the diesel engine gave its usual reluctant rattle, then roared into noisy life.

Dad's always threatening to get rid of the truck. Costs too much to run, he says. Takes too much time to maintain. Thing is, though, we need it, even though we're a three-car family—according to Dad. The truck. Mum's car—a beat-up old jalopy she's had ever since I can remember. It was bright yellow once, but now it's faded to a kind of buttery cream. Dad says it's held together with rubber bands and bits of string; Mum says it gives a tenth the amount of trouble his truck does. That's how it got its name, I guess: Rubber Band.

Nick and me—we live in dread of Dad finally deciding to get rid of the truck or Rubber Band. Because then we'd be down to the third "car." And being taken to soccer on Saturdays in *that*—no way!

Dad pulled out into the traffic. The car he cut in front of gave a disgruntled honk, but Dad ignored it. He turned to me, one big hand on the wheel, the other elbow leaning out of the open window. Freezing air rushed in, turning my bare knees to ice. Dad never seems to look where he's going when he drives—not like Mum, who keeps both eyes on the road even when she's talking. Dad roars around like he owns the road; Mum keeps a constant check on the speedometer. Yet Mum's had any number of bumps and speeding tickets, and Dad leads what he calls a "charmed life." Or claims to.

Taking his hand off the steering wheel, he glanced at his watch. "Ten to twelve, Son." He shot me a glance. I knew what was coming.

Dad has this real bushy black mustache, which makes it almost impossible to tell what mood he's in, or what he's thinking. He doesn't smile like other dads; or if he does, it doesn't show. The barometer to Dad's moods is his eyes. He has these deep, crinkly wrinkles around them . . . like everything with Dad, it's hard to explain unless you know him.

When I was little we got these two bath toys for Christmas. They're long gone now, and nothing more than lumps of plastic, when it came down to it, but I've never forgotten them. Dumb, huh? Way back, the bath toys had bubble bath in them. A bright green plastic fish for Nick, full of green bubble bath. And for me, a pale blue whale, with blue bubble bath. Even after the bubble bath was finished, we still played with the containers in the bath. I was only about six, which would've made Nick eight. Anyhow, there was something about my whale. He had these deep, smiley wrinkles—this magic whaley smile—that just exactly reminded me of Dad on a good day.

Years later, I realized I hadn't seen Whaley for a while. I asked Mum where he was. "What, that old thing? I threw it out ages ago, Pippin—things like that aren't meant to last forever. And anyway, it was full of mold."

Right now Dad's wrinkle barometer was set to *fine and sunny*, and he was beaming me his best whaley smile. "Yup—ten to twelve," he repeated. "Know what I feel like,

Son?" Of course I knew. He said the exact same thing every weekend it was his turn to take me to soccer.

"What, Dad?"

"An ice cream! Whaddaya say, Son? A quick trip to the Dairy Den, just you and me. An extra special treat—no need to mention it to your mother or Nick."

I guess every family has its own shorthand—stuff you say, and your mum and dad and brother know exactly what's behind it . . . but no one else would, not in a million years. In McLeod family shorthand, where our ritual trip to the Dairy Den was concerned, *no need to mention it to your mother* meant a whole bunch of things. With lunch half an hour away, Mum would go ballistic if she knew we were eating ice creams. Plus, the whole family was on a tight budget that didn't allow for luxuries like ice cream—except on really special occasions.

And last—but as far as Mum was concerned, most important of all—was Dad's cholesterol. He'd had it checked out a couple of years back, and it was sky high. For months Mum tiptoed around him, like she expected any moment he'd have a sudden rush of cholesterol to the brain and keel over dead. Gradually, life returned to normal—if you can call no fry-ups, no ice cream, and no fish and chips "normal."

Without waiting for an answer, Dad flipped a U-turn and headed for the mall. There was an empty space right outside the Dairy Den. Dad pulled in, turned off the engine, and beamed over at me. "Now, Son, let's think." The smile vanished. Frowning, he pretended to consider. "I reckon business-wise, this week's been . . . hmmm . . . a . . . *two-topping week!" Every* week was a two-topping week, but every week he said that—always played it out, keeping me in suspense (not!), while he pretended to run through the week's deliveries in his mind.

We both chose soft-serve cones. Dad always had the same thing: an ice cream with a chocolate cone and chopped nuts. Not me. This time, I had a choc dip with hundreds and thousands of sprinkles. If they dipped it for long enough, and then sprinkled the hundreds and thousands on straightaway, heaps of them stuck on. Today, the girl behind the counter did it just right.

The tight knot in my middle was gradually beginning to loosen. I watched Dad take a massive bite off the top of his ice cream, starting the truck with the other hand. The cone stuck out of his mouth like a fat cigar. Reversing, he let go of the steering wheel and grabbed the cone between his thumb and forefinger. When he crunched down, shards of chocolate flew everywhere.

I started to nibble the edges of my dip. That's how I like to eat it—levering the thin coating of chocolate off piece by piece, until only the plain ice cream is left.

"Don't nibble; you'll make a mess," growled Dad, eyes on the road for once.

We were turning off the highway onto the Hillcrest ramp when I finally got down to the plain ice cream. Dad had the radio on the sports program, but it was basketball, so it was turned real low. His cone was long gone. He was beating a gentle tattoo on the steering wheel, as relaxed as he ever was.

I thought back to the game—to the man on the sideline. He could have been anyone; could have been a stranger. But he wasn't—he was my dad.

My ice cream was melting. I did one of my special hi-tech circular slurps to collect the drips. There can't have been more than a tablespoon of ice cream in that slurp, but it sat in my stomach like lead.

He was my dad. Surely I could talk to him? If I could only find a way to begin, surely he would understand . . .

"Dad . . ."

A sideways whaley smile. "Yup, Son?"

"Dad . . . I wish . . . You know at soccer? The game? I wish . . ."

"Wish what, Son?"

"I wish I could be more like the other kids. You . . . that you'd be . . ."

"More like the other parents?" The smile was still there. The wrinkles were deeper. It was going to be okay. "We're all different, Son."

"Yeah, but Dad—you know how you always stand apart . . . they . . . *they* always stand apart . . . from you? It's because . . . well . . . to them, it's the game that counts. How it's played, not the result. And the ref—what the ref says, goes. Dad . . ."

I was almost whispering now. Hardly daring to look, I slid a glance at him. He was watching the road, frowning, but listening, thinking about what I was saying.

DAD

I plowed on. "Dad—sometimes I dread soccer on Saturdays." *Always dread it*; but I didn't need to say that. "I like you coming to watch; I really do." *Liar.* "But I wish you'd stay out of the game. Just be a spectator, like the other dads. Be proud of me for what I do right—there must be *some* things, surely?" Tears were clogging my throat. I didn't dare say: *Be proud of me for who I am.*

I didn't dare say any of it.

"Dad . . ."

A sideways whaley smile. "Yup, Son?"

"Dad . . . I wish . . . You know at soccer? The game? I wish . . ."

"You wish that goal had gone in? I know. You're not my son for nothing. Still, there's always next time. That's the great thing about being thirteen, with a dad who knows the game and is there to support you, through thick and thin. Now finish that ice cream—we're almost home."

MY BABY SISTER

We wound up the hill and turned into Contour Terrace. Dad pulled into our driveway, narrowly missing the battered old ride-on fire engine outside the garage. "Bring that in with you, Son—there'll be hell to pay if someone drives over it. And don't forget your gear."

Rubber Band was already home—that meant lunch would soon be ready. I gathered up my stuff: filthy cleats, bag, drink bottle. Also Dad's parka, and the fire engine, hooking it up by the handle with my little finger. Dad had left the front door ajar, and I shouldered my way in.

Instantly, there was a thundering sound, like the "Charge of the Light Brigade" in that poem Mrs. Holland read us in English. I put down all the stuff and braced myself. Around the corner, at breakneck speed, crawled my baby sister. She's not how you'd imagine a baby girl of a year and a half. You'd think: baby sister? Cute little thing in a pink frilly dress with golden ringlets, all coos and gurgles and big blue eyes.

You'd be wrong.

MY BABY SISTER

Madeline Estella was a surprise from the first moment we found out about her. Like Nick and me, she's named after characters in novels by Charles Dickens. Mum used to be an English teacher, and he's her favorite author. Even now, in the evenings when the rest of us are watching TV, Mum'll have her nose in a book. I'm a bit like that, too—I guess she's where I get it from. So when Nick was born, he was christened Nicholas David. Two years later, along I came. Philip Joseph. As Nick says, it could have been worse. Oliver Twist and Tiny Tim, for instance.

Eleven years on, I guess we all pretty much figured the family was complete. But one evening, just as Nick was slouching off to his room and I was heading for the television, Mum called us back into the kitchen. She was sitting at the table, and Dad was rattling away in the corner cupboard, with his back to us. "Jim," said Mum, "stop fidgeting and come and sit down." Nick and me looked at each other. Something weird was going on. Mum had this kind of secretive look, a deep-down glimmer of excitement—and something else, something deep and shining I'd never seen in her eyes before. Dad came to the table and sat down, meek as a lamb.

"Boys," said Mum, "Dad and I have some news. It's something important; something wonderful."

The two of them exchanged a glance. It seemed to crackle in the air with a kind of private electricity, making me want to look away as if I'd blundered in somewhere I didn't belong. The smile wrinkles around Dad's eyes deepened into curving crescents. He covered

Mum's slim pale hand with his strong brown one.

"You tell them, Jim," she said softly.

"Your mother and I . . ." Dad began, frowning sternly, his voice extra-deep and gruff-sounding. He cleared his throat loudly. "Your mother . . ."

There was a pause. We all waited. Then Mum laughed. "We're going to have another baby."

I felt as if the Earth had stopped spinning. Looking at Nick, I knew I must have the same look on my face he did— open-mouthed shock.

Mum was carrying on, her voice matter-of-fact. "You're both old enough to realize this wasn't planned. Sometimes, things happen unexpectedly. And when they do, even though you're very surprised at first, they often turn out to be the best things of all. This will be one of them. Financially, it won't be easy. But we'll manage somehow. And one thing's for sure: there'll always be enough love for everyone."

She came around the table and gave first me, then Nick, a hug and a kiss. Nick rubbed his away automatically. He had a strange look on his face. Kind of shy; wary, almost. He was blushing—Nick was actually blushing! "Mum," he said. His voice had broken by that stage, but it came out in a funny squeak. "Mu-um—what am I going to tell my friends? They'll find out sooner or later. You guys . . . it's so *embarrassing*."

"Nicholas . . ." rumbled Dad warningly.

But for once, Nick ignored him. "I mean . . . no one else's mum and dad . . . parents *don't* . . . oh, jeez. What a gross-out."

I slid a glance at Dad, waiting for the inevitable explosion; for Nick to be sent to his room in disgrace. Dad's mustache bristled; who knew what it was hiding? But one thing was for sure: no one could have missed the laughter in his eyes as he gave Mum a slow, deliberate wink.

As for me, I couldn't help having just one quick look at Mum's stomach, covered by her washed-out, old flowery apron. Under there—somewhere in there—was a new baby brother or sister. It couldn't be true . . . yet I knew it was.

Six months later, Madeline was born.

We went to see her in the hospital before she was even a day old. There she was, a real person, brand new. She had a bright red face and a shock of sticky-up black hair, and her eyes were screwed tight shut against the world. She was bundled up in a yellow blanket, and Dad was holding her as if she were made of glass, with this extra-stern look on his face. Mum was propped up in bed, surrounded by flowers. She was pale, but her eyes were very bright. "Let the boys hold her, Jim," she told Dad. "Go on, Nick . . . Pip. She's a lot tougher than she looks. She won't break."

Nick put his hands behind his back and shook his head. He felt the way I did, I could tell. But I looked at Mum's face, and I heard myself say, "Okay. I'll have a go. Just . . . don't be mad if I drop it . . . her, I mean."

Straightaway, Dad started fussing. He sat me down in the one visitor's chair—so if I did drop her, at least she wouldn't fall far. Then he lowered the yellow bundle carefully into my arms. Nick watched narrowly from beside the door. "You have to support her head, Son," Dad told me. "If you don't, it'll fall off."

She was so light! Already, she smelt of the tiny spare room at home—the baby's room—even though she hadn't even been there yet. I stared down at her. I couldn't stop looking.

Then suddenly she opened her eyes. Just the tiniest slit— the darkest eyes I'd ever seen. Eyes dark as Dad's . . . dark as Nick's. She had their same level, dark eyebrows; their same black hair. She looked straight up at me. Well, almost straight—she had this funny squint. Instantly, I started worrying for her. What if it never went away?

"Who knows what she'll make of her life?" Dad was musing. "A Grand Slam champion . . . an Olympic gymnast? All in there, just waiting to happen."

My heart twisted with fear for her. Surely it was enough that she was here at all, so small and perfect? She squinted up at me . . . and smiled. And right then I knew she wasn't like Dad, or Nick. She was like me.

"That's not a real smile; it's only wind," Dad told us.

Truth was, I hardly even heard him. I was too busy smiling back at my new baby sister.

MAKE DAD MAD

And now, a year and a half later, here was Madeline, World Champion Crawler, thundering toward me at the speed of light, like one of those battery-powered toys that goes and goes and keeps on going. Plopping back on her butt, reaching up her arms to be picked up. "Biffin! Uppy!"

I scooped her up in one arm, gave her a kiss, and carried her through to the kitchen, where I put her into her highchair.

Mum was at the stove, stirring the soup. In winter, Saturday was soup day—Mum made it in advance, and heated it up in the big black saucepan when we came in from soccer. Some days it was proper soup, from a real recipe— pumpkin and coriander, or tomato and basil, or cream of chicken. Other times, though, it'd just be a "Mum Special"—made from whatever bits and pieces needed to be used up. "Rule number one when you're cooking," she'd say: "if you put nice things in, it can't possibly turn out nasty." It was true, too. Mum Specials were everyone's favorite—and they never turned out the same twice running.

Mum glanced up from the stove and smiled. "Give Dad and Nick a shout, would you, Pippin? How was your game? Have fun?"

"Yeah, kind of," I mumbled.

Mum laid out huge, steaming bowls of soup with a basket of crusty wholegrain rolls. In slouched Nick, on a waft of wintergreen. He's always getting injured . . . or claiming to. He slid into his chair, reached over to Madeline's special table, and helped himself to a generous pinch of her raisins. She frowned at him, just like Dad minus the mustache. "No more daisin," she announced.

"Hey, Pipsqueak," Nick said to me. "Howdja go? Didja win?"

"Yup. Three-two."

"Score any goals?"

I hesitated. "Nah." Thought for a second, remembering the run that had ended in disaster. Quick check—no sign of Dad. "I nearly did, though."

There was a snort as Dad came in and took his place at the head of the table. He gave me a shrewd glint from under his eyebrows, but didn't say anything. He helped himself to a roll, picked up his spoon, and took a rapid slurp of soup. I filled my spoon, too, and blew in it.

He shot a glance over at Nick. "Well?"

"We won. Four-nil." There was a pause, but I knew he hadn't finished. Not Nick. "I scored a hat trick." My brother looked down modestly for a beat. I stared at the curls of steam rising off my spoon. Then he was off. "Hey, Dad, I wish you'd'a been there! You should've seen that first goal! I made it myself—solo all the way, man! Plus, I scored it left-footed. *Wham!* Right between the goalie's legs! You should've seen his face!" He ripped off a huge bite of roll. His eyes were blazing; he took a couple of quick chews, swallowed half, and carried on: "The second one was even better, though. I—"

"Blnt blawk murf boor bouf bull," said Dad through a mouthful of bread.

Nick shot a quick glance at me. Family shorthand. Finished chewing, swallowed, and was off again. I sighed, and choked down another spoonful. It was a classic Mum Special, but I wasn't hungry.

Watching Nick rearrange the salt and pepper and margarine to represent the defenders he'd barreled through, I could see just how Dad must have been at the same age. Strong features, handsome in Dad—even I could see that—but still overgrown and gawky in my brother. Ears like jug handles; a nose just a bit too big, sporting a large pimple on one side; a square chin; dark eyes under straight, black brows.

Long ago, when we first moved into Contour Terrace, the Woods came over with a casserole to introduce themselves and welcome us to the neighborhood. Dad was still on crutches, in pain a lot, and grumpy as hell with Nick and me. But meeting the Woods, he was all sweetness and light—much to Mum's relief. I can still remember what he said, even though it was years ago: "These are my two boys, Nick and Pip. Nick's the ace sportsman—the son I always thought

I'd have. As for Pip . . . well, he's his mother's boy, I guess. Nose in a book and head in the clouds."

The worst part was that it was true. Then . . . and now. I do take after Mum—not just in the things I'm good at, but how I look. I've got her same soft, floppy blond hair, her narrow face and green eyes. Where Nick has smooth olive skin that tans in a day, I have Mum's fine pale skin. Mum and me stand side by side in the bathroom slathering on sunscreen while Dad and Nick pace up and down outside, grumbling about being late. And still my nose turns pink and starts to peel.

Nick is Dad's son all right. But it hurt to hear him say it.

The other thing about Nick: close as he is to Dad, he knows exactly the right buttons to press to wind him up—and he's not scared of doing it, either. Like last school holidays, when he entered the *Make Dad Mad* competition.

"I saw the ball coming off the corner kick," Nick was going on. "It was this high, floating ball—a perfect corner, just like we've been practicing. Everyone jumped for it—but I barged the defender with my shoulder in midair and knocked him off the ball. I connected with it just right, with the top of my forehead. Say this is the ball, Dad, and I'm here, right? It came . . ."

Yeah . . . *Make Dad Mad*. Nick has this real off-the-wall sense of humor. Sometimes, it gets him into trouble. More and more, he doesn't seem to care.

He'd been wanting the new Black Attack CD for months. Didn't have a hope of getting it, though. Then the radio station he listens to had one of their holiday specials. Every day, around the same time, they invited listeners to phone in and put a call through to their dads at work. If you could make your dad mad, live on the radio with half the world listening, you got to win a CD. Not just any CD. The new Black Attack CD—the one Nick would sell his soul to have.

Nick had planned to spend the day with his friend Mark, down in Greendale. They were going to catch the bus into town, hang out, get together with some friends. Maybe arrange a kick-around on the school sports field. "Get rid of some of that energy, Mum," he said innocently.

But heading out the door, he hissed in my ear, "Hey, Pipsqueak. Want a laugh? Then listen in to Outer Limit at eleven—you can use my radio, but keep your sticky fingers off the stuff in my room. I'll know if you touch anything. Especially Horace."

My brother's the only guy I know with the head of a red deer on the wall of his room, complete with glass eyes and antlers like hat racks. A deer he shot himself. Nick and Dad went off hunting together about the time Nick's voice started to change. "Man's stuff," Dad said.

"Male bonding," teased Mum, but we could all tell she was pleased.

As for Nick, he'd walked on air for weeks before, lording it over me as he described the trips to the rifle range, the smell of gunpowder, the kick of the butt when he fired. He even showed me the bruise it left in the hollow beside his bony shoulder.

"You'll get your turn one day, Son," Dad promised,

ruffling my hair through the truck window.

When they returned three days later, out of the back of the truck had come Horace, the hack marks still raw on his neck, his eyes milky and opaque, and his tongue lolling. Looking at Horace and seeing the expression on my brother's face, I began to understand what it was all about. Somehow, in those three days, Nick stopped being a kid. It was as if he'd crossed an invisible boundary to the side where Dad belonged; there was Horace up on his wall, to make sure none of us forgot.

And there I was, at quarter to eleven, in the middle of the floor in Nick's room, the radio on real soft so Dad wouldn't hear, and Horace glaring down at me. If Dad knew I was in Nick's room, I'd catch it—he'd never believe Nick said I could be there.

Dad was in the kitchen organizing the orders for the evening's run, and Mum had taken Madeline to morning tea with some friends.

Ten to . . . five to—and at last, at two minutes to eleven, on came Jase the DJ: "Here's the moment you've all been waiting for—*Make Dad Mad!* Your chance to make *your* dad raving, spitting, swearing mad *live on air* and win a copy of the new Black Attack CD, *Nightstick*. And we have a caller on air: Nick. How are ya, Nick?"

"Hi, Jase," came my brother's voice out of his radio, sounding way different from normal and at the same time weirdly familiar. I couldn't believe my ears. Was he crazy?

"Now, Nick," said Jase, "you have a plan to make your

dad really, really mad this morning; is that right?"

"Yup, right," said Nick. I could hear someone laughing in the background.

"And you're sure you can do it?"

"Sure I'm sure." Confident as only Nick can be.

"And you realize we've had the crashed car? We've had the broken window? We've even had the house burning down?"

"Yeah, I know. I've got something new."

"Well, you sure sound confident, Nick. You sound like a guy who knows the score . . . a guy who's got what it takes to make his dad really, really mad—and handle the consequences. You're sure you want to go ahead?"

"I'm sure." Nick *really* wanted that CD.

"Okay, let's do it. I'm dialing the number; I'm hearing it ring."

In the kitchen, I heard our phone start to ring.

Dad's voice: "Philip! *Get that phone!*"

Ring . . . ring . . . ring . . .

"Philip!"

Jase: "He isn't home."

A whisper from Nick: "He's home."

Ring . . . ring . . .

At last, Dad's growl over the radio: "McLeod."

Nick, suddenly sounding very young. "Dad? Hi—it's me. Nick."

A grunt from Dad.

Nick: "Dad—I'm at Mark's. But Mum—she asked me to

tell you this morning, before she left. I forgot; that's why I'm phoning. She wants you to do the shopping. Because, you know, she's tied up with the baby at that tea thing." My heart skipped a beat. Nick had made his first mistake. Dad would realize something was up for sure—no one ever called Madeline "the baby" anymore.

But Dad didn't seem to notice. "How much is there? Did she say?"

"Not a lot. The list's up where it always is—on the fridge door."

Well, if asking Dad to do the shopping was supposed to make him stark, staring, raving mad, it didn't seem to be working. Some days it might, I had to admit—but not today. I sensed a zillion listeners waiting for Nick to push whichever button it took to make Dad go off.

"Okay, okay," grumbled Dad. "I'll do it."

"But wait, Dad, wait!" yelped Nick, desperate to catch Dad before he hung up—Dad never winds a conversation down and says "good-bye," like other people. "Mum said to ask you to add one more thing—to be sure not to forget."

Dad has a memory like a sieve—it's a family legend. Along with the rest of the country, I listened to Dad scraping his chair back and lumbering over to the fridge with the phone, to write the extra thing onto the list.

"Well?"

"It's . . . ummm . . . peanut butter, Dad. Smooth, not crunchy."

I could picture Dad taking the list down, hunting for a

pen. Running his eye over the list to get a fix on how long it would take him.

With my heart in my mouth, I listened as Dad read the contents of our shopping list out on the air. We all added things to the list—stuff we really needed, or luxuries we hoped Mum might stretch the budget to that week. With me, those were usually Jelly Wobbles. With Nick, it was things he knew we weren't allowed, like gum, or could never afford and didn't even want, like smoked salmon and caviar.

Nick must have added something to the list. But what?

"Sausages," read Dad. "Eggs. Tissues. Flour. Potatoes. Jelly Wobbles—I'm not getting those; Pip can forget it." Sitting there on Nick's floor, I blushed. "Dishwashing powder. Cuh . . . cuh . . . *condoms?*"

"Oh, jeez, Dad—I forgot that was on the list!"

"Condoms!"

"Look, Dad, sorry—forget it, okay? I have to go!"

"*Nicholas!* Don't you dare hang up! What the hell is the meaning of this? Why the hell are you putting *condoms* on your mother's shopping list?"

"Dad . . . I . . ."

"You what? You bloody *what*? What the hell do you think you're doing? And how dare you ask your *mother*—how—what—you're *fifteen*!"

Nick, battling to sound subdued, struggling not to crack up laughing: "Dad—are you mad?"

"Mad?" yelled Dad. "Of course I'm not mad! You get your backside home right now, and I'll show you just how *not* mad I am. And if you're not home in half an hour, I'm coming to get you!"

The phone slammed down. An electric silence rang through our house, and the houses of a zillion listeners around New Zealand.

There was a definite note of awe in Jase's voice when he finally spoke. "Well, Nick, looks like you nailed it. That CD's on its way to you, no questions asked. Sounds like you're one young man who knows how to make his dad really, *reeeeally* mad. And now, just to get you off the hook, we'll call back and let your dad know it's all just a joke. It's the least we can do for you, mate."

Nick, panic-stricken: "No, Jase—please, *no!*"

Too late. In the kitchen, the phone rang once. "What!" barks Dad.

Jase, every inch the jolly DJ: "Hi there, Nick's Dad! This is Jase from Outer Limit radio station. Just a quick call to let you know you can relax—you're not about to become a grandpa! It's all a joke—and thank you for being live on air on Outer Limit!"

That was when I knew Nick wouldn't be around for the next few days—kind of like Salman Rushdie, that writer guy Mrs. Holland told us about who had to go into hiding to save his skin. Because however mad Dad had been before, knowing he'd been made a fool of on national radio . . . well, that meant Nick was dead meat, pure and simple.

It was over a week before I heard Dad telling the story to

Mr. Wood, and laughing about it. "One thing about that boy of mine," bragged Dad, "he's got guts. And when it comes down to it, it's guts that make you a winner."

Nick had chalked that one up as a major success—but then, not content to leave it at that, he tried to follow it up by pulling a variation on Mum. I'd snuck into the kitchen and copied the list out again in my best writing, minus the condoms, so Mum wouldn't see. But on the next week's list, Nick wrote it down again: *Condoms*. Right under where I'd written *Toothpaste*.

We both knew Mum would see it before Dad got home. She'd see it—but what would she do?

I was in the kitchen when Mum crossed over to the fridge with Madeline on her hip and a pen in her hand. I saw her read; hesitate; smile. Then write something on the list. Something too long to be *Rice* or *Sugar*.

Soon as she left the room, I went over and snuck a peek.

We were both at the kitchen table when Nick walked in. Mum doing Dad's accounts, her half-moon specs perched on her nose and Madeline playing happily on the floor beside her; me pretending to read. I watched from over my book as Nick sauntered oh-so-casually up to the fridge. Mum was watching, too, out of the corner of her eye. Grinning at his own cleverness, Nick read what she'd written: *What size?*

I had watched the smirk slowly fade from my brother's face. It was replaced by a look of uncertainty. I could almost hear him thinking: *What size? Do they come in different sizes?* And then: *What size am I? What size . . . what size should I be?*

Nick didn't have to try too hard to stay a giant leap ahead of Dad; but Mum . . . well, Mum managed to stay a hop, skip, and a jump ahead of Nick, no problem.

THE FIRST MANDARIN

Okay, okay, there's this girl. But no one knows—and I mean *no one*. Especially not her. It's Katie Wood, the girl next door. How corny can you get?

I've known her forever. When we first moved into Contour Terrace, she was just a kid my own age who happened to be a girl. Not much of a girl, to be honest—more of an honorary boy. She had a round, friendly face, with long hair in pigtails, blond on top and darker underneath, where the sun didn't reach. That made the segments of pigtail kind of patchwork blond and dark like a wooden chessboard, as if they belonged to two totally different people. She had sparkly blue eyes and long legs—even then—and scabby, knobbly knees. She always wore scruffy shorts and a T-shirt, except when we were at school. A total tomboy, and the best friend I'd ever had.

We were always at each other's houses . . . and when we weren't, we'd be hunkered down at the fence, talking through it, hatching plots or sharing sweets. We were in the same class at school and on the same soccer team.

Then one day a year back, things suddenly changed.

Our two families were at a picnic, and we were playing a game of tag—kids' stuff, but everyone was feeling pretty silly. I was It; I'd been going after Katie all afternoon, but I hadn't managed to get so much as a finger on her. She was like a gazelle—she'd kind of shot up and thinned down . . . in some places, anyhow. She kept slipping away from me, ducking and dodging and laughing. It was driving me crazy. Then, at last, I got her out into the open and ran her down. Did a flying tackle and grabbed her by the ankle. She crashed down onto the grass with me beside her. Rolled over, winded, hair all over the place, tears of laughter in her eyes. I looked down into her face . . . and in that instant, every-thing changed. It was like someone flicked a switch deep down inside.

Click.

Quickly, I got up and dusted myself down. I didn't hold out a hand to help her up, like I would have five seconds before. Instead I yelled, "You're It!" and took off like a rocket. But no matter how fast I ran, I couldn't outrun that strange, terrifying new feeling. As time went on, I didn't want to.

At school we kept our distance. But in cooking class we had to have partners, and Miss Carling made us have girls. And somehow, it just turned out that Katie was my partner.

I reckon pairing girls and boys was Miss Carling's way of trying to prevent cooking class from turning into a national disaster—which it probably would if you had two boys working together. With some of the guys in my class, it'd be almost a point of honor to mess up. Unfortunately, though, she hadn't reckoned with Katie, still a tomboy even though she'd stopped looking the part, and hardly able to boil water without burning it. I wasn't much better.

Monday was double cooking, double English, then break—the best possible way to start the week. Today we were making Swiss rolls. First off, we covered the theory— all about how sifting the flour incorporates air which helps make the mixture rise; the importance of keeping the oven closed during the baking process (Miss Carling's pretty big on high-tech terminology like "the baking process")—all that kind of thing. Old Carling's not how you'd imagine a cooking teacher to be. She's the kind of person who probably would have been happier as a prison officer. She has a narrow, pinched face, and a mouth like a shark. And she has this wart on her chin, with a single hair growing out of it. It gives you something to think about in the theory lessons— how someone can look in the mirror, day after day, and have the self-control not to tweak that hair out. But that's the Carling—tough as old boots. Barely human.

Painstakingly, we copied the recipe into our folders, right after apple crumble.

At last, it was time to put our books away. Katie gave me a grin and a wink. She headed off to collect the ingredients while I went to the storeroom to gather the utensils.

One thing about Katie, past disasters never shake her

confidence. Standing at our table whisking the eggs and sugar, taking turns when our hands felt like they were about to snap off, she shot me one of her shimmering smiles. "Hard to believe this will soon be a *pale golden, springy* Swiss roll, isn't it, Piphead?" she said, quoting from the recipe.

It was even harder to believe when we poured the mixture into the tin. "It looks awful watery," I said doubtfully.

"Nonsense," scoffed Katie. "Have faith, Pip. Have faith in the Carling, the laws of Home Economics, and the magic of the Baking Process. Think of all that whisking, how much air it must have incorporated. Fix your tiny mind on the thought of a fresh Swiss roll at break, instead of soggy sandwiches! Come on, let's reverently slide it into the oven, taking care not to bang the door, and get on with the washing-up. And guess whose turn it is to wash?"

Mine, of course. I ran a sink full of hot, sudsy water and made a start. Katie carried the stuff over from our table; but for once, she was having her work cut out to keep up with me. I glanced over my shoulder to see where she'd got to.

Then suddenly she was beside me. "Pip," she hissed, "Pip, come quick! Hurry, before the Carling sees."

My heart thumped into my shoes. Something must have gone badly wrong. But what?

Shooting a quick glance over at the Carling, who was marking our homework assignments at her desk, I followed Katie over to our table. There were still a couple of plastic bowls on it, but apart from that, everything looked fine.

"You haven't opened the oven door, have you?" I whispered. She shook her head wordlessly. "Then *what*?"

"Shhhh." With another quick check on Carling, she lifted the plate resting on top of one of the mixing bowls. For a second I thought she'd caught something in there—a cockroach, maybe. That would be just like Katie. She'd caught something and was scared it might leap out. I squinted warily through the crack.

The bowl was full of flour.

"Huh?"

Katie pulled a desperate face. "The *flour*, Piphead. Don't you *see*?"

I didn't. "See what? Where did you get this from?"

She rolled her eyes. "This," she pointed, "is the *flour* we should have folded into the mixture 'as lightly as possible with a metal spoon'—but we didn't!"

Light dawned. "But, Katie . . . didn't you . . ."

"But Pip, didn't *you*?" she echoed. "The answer is no. No squared. And the question," she went on, a smile quivering at the corners of her mouth, her eyes dancing, "the million-dollar question is: what the heck are we going to do now?"

In the end, under conditions of the utmost secrecy, I buried the flour in the depths of the trash bin, while Katie created a diversion by allowing our sink to overflow. We mopped up the mess, finished tidying up, and listened to a long lecture on "responsibility in the kitchen" . . . and then it was time to take our Swiss roll out of the oven.

We went across the room together. It seemed a longer

walk than usual. On the way we passed Paul and Melissa, bearing their perfect Swiss roll back to their table. It had risen right up above the edges of the tin. It was the exact shade of pale gold I'd imagined. It even had the crispy edges the Carling said might need trimming off with a sharp knife. Melissa gave us a smug smile.

Katie and I hovered at the oven door. "After you," I told her.

"No, after *you*."

We exchanged a grin. We'd been through worse. Together, we opened the oven door. Lifted the cake tin out. Stared at it in horrified disbelief. I suppose somehow, at the back of my mind, I'd hoped it might look . . . well . . . almost okay. But it didn't.

Doing our best to shield the contents of our tin from prying eyes, we hurried back to our table. Quickly, we turned it out onto the tea towel we had ready, sprinkled with sugar. It was as heavy as lead—the exact consistency of wet leather. We stripped off the lining paper and quickly rolled up the tea towel. Just in time.

The Carling cruised past, doing her rounds. She gave us a suspicious look. "What about you two? Everything all right?"

"Yes, Miss Carling," we chorused.

She returned to the front of the room. "Right, boys and girls: we have ten minutes left. Collect your jam; unroll your sponges, spread them evenly, re-roll, and then I want to see them all on the cooling racks at the front of the classroom for grading. Quickly, now."

Grim-faced, Katie followed the instructions. In my usual role of assistant chef, I fetched and carried and concealed our disaster as best I could. Daintily, Katie sprinkled a final dusting of sugar over the top. We exchanged one last glance. I felt like one of those guys in the French Revolution, headed for the guillotine. Bravely, we bore our Swiss roll to the front table, and set it down beside the others.

A titter ran through the classroom. We stepped back and took our place with the rest of the class. Up marched the Carling, grade book in her hand. She looked at the table, and froze. There lay ten perfect Swiss rolls, fat and golden and dusted with sugar. And beside them skulked a poor, sad, floppy sausage, less than a quarter their size, its ends drooping.

Carling looked straight at us. "Well?" she barked. "What happened this time?"

"I don't know, Miss Carling," I mumbled.

"Did you add the flour?"

Katie bit her lip. "Flour? The flour? Pip—did you add the flour?"

"The flour? Uh—I don't really remember putting it in, no. I thought . . . that *you* might be putting the flour in, Katie."

"Kathryn, Philip: you both have a zero for this assignment. And in addition, a detention." She glanced at the dreaded grade book. "You should be aware that at present, your cumulative mark for the year rests on twenty percent. I need hardly remind you that less than fifty percent constitutes a fail. The rest of you may collect your work, in time for morning break. Kathryn and Philip, you may . . . *dispose* of yours now. Class dismissed."

For once we didn't split up straight after class. Instead we walked to English together, Katie swinging her bag, in high spirits. It takes a lot to get Katie down. "Tell you one thing about our Swiss roll, Piphead," she said, "it may not have been the best, but it had character. And there's a lot to be said for that."

English is my favorite subject. I'm good at it, too. And Mrs. Holland is really cool. She's this sturdy—well, the other kids call her fat—lady with untidy brown hair and a broad, warm, beaming face. Her cheeks are ruddy, and her eyes are really bright. When she gets going about something— some writer, or a poem we're studying—she fizzes with enthusiasm, like a sparkler on Guy Fawkes night. Mrs. Holland's lessons are always interesting. Sometimes it's hard to see what they have to do with English, but they always hop from one thing to another before anyone has a chance to get bored.

She was waiting at the front of the class as we all straggled in. We pulled out our chairs, shuffled, and settled. We all looked at her expectantly, waiting to be told which textbook to take out.

Instead, she produced a soft cloth bag from her desk drawer. We shifted in our seats and craned our necks, wondering what was inside.

"I thought we'd try something different this morning.

Start the new week with a challenge." She tipped the bag upside down over her desk. Out fell five small, soft, brightly colored balls. They were quartered like oranges in segments of red, yellow, green, and blue, and looked as if they might be made of soft leather. "Juggling. Can anyone here juggle?" Up went a tentative hand—Michael Roberts, my official school best friend. "Michael? Would you like to come up and show us?"

Michael mooched up to the front of the class and stood there, looking self-conscious. He picked up two of the balls, and tossed one up in the air. Quickly, with a kind of sideways shuffle, he slipped the other ball into his free hand, then caught the first one as it came down. He did this a couple of times, to ironic claps and whistles from the rest of the class. Then he looked over at Mrs. Holland for approval.

She raised one eyebrow. "Not bad. Not bad at all. Thank you, Michael. Now, what do we all think of when we think of juggling?" Hands went up around the room. Clowns. Circuses. Jesters. The Middle Ages. The class was really buzzing.

Ten minutes into the lesson, Shaun Wilson put up his hand. He was always the first to rock the boat and ask awkward questions, trying to trip up the teachers. "Mrs. Holland," he asked, "can *you* juggle?"

"Can I juggle?" she repeated, smiling across at him. "Before I answer your question, Shaun, let me tell you all something. Everyone who is able to juggle three balls for twenty seconds by the last Friday of term—in three weeks time—will receive a ten-dollar snack-shop voucher. Three balls; three weeks; ten dollars." A ripple ran around the room. "There'll also be a special prize, awarded at my discretion."

She paused; rested her fingertips on the bag lying on her desk. "My juggling balls. It'll have to be well earned; I'm not parting with them lightly. But the most valuable prize of all will be the satisfaction of acquiring a new skill—one I guarantee each and every one of you is capable of learning, with a bit of determination and a lot of patience." Her eyes twinkled. "I know you'll find it's worth the effort. Think about it: almost everyone's impressed by a competent display of juggling. It's a cool party trick." Shaun glanced back at Simon, and winked. I could tell he thought Mrs. Holland was fudging—hoping we'd forget what he'd asked. I wasn't so sure. "More than that, juggling is an art form. Juggling is a *life skill*."

With that, she picked up the five balls and moved to the center of the room, where she stood, feet firmly planted. Her eyes moved around the class. There was absolute silence. I hoped she wasn't going to make a fool of herself . . . but somehow, I doubted she would.

One after the other, the colored balls rose into the air. First one, then two, then three, four . . . and finally, all five were dancing in an intricate pattern, on . . . and on . . . and on.

And then Mrs. Holland was catching them again: one, two, three, four, five. Without dropping a single one.

Applause broke out around the room; people were tilting back on their chairs, grinning across at each other.

As for Mrs. Holland, her eyes were glowing, and her cheeks were even pinker than usual. She slipped the balls back in the bag. "And now, it's time for some more serious business. Will you all take out your poetry books, and turn to page forty-one, please."

I headed home on my bike after school, the image of those balls still dancing in my mind. I was determined to be up at the front of the class on the last day of term, juggling three balls. Imagine winning those juggling balls! And a ten-dollar snack-shop voucher . . . There were kids who bought them by the handful, and headed to the shop every lunch time. There were kids who had money on Fridays, or at the end of term. And then there were kids like me.

Already, I knew exactly what I'd get. There were these giant licorice—cube-shaped, with pink and green layers separated by thin strips of licorice. Paul had given me one once, when I'd helped him with his homework. I'd peeled it apart and eaten it layer by layer. I'd made it last almost a whole lunch time. Even now, if I closed my eyes, I could still taste that smoky, aniseed sweetness on my tongue.

But it was more than the voucher . . . more even than the juggling balls. It was what Mrs. Holland had said about a new challenge: a life skill. *Almost everyone's impressed by a competent display of juggling.*

I was going to learn to juggle, no matter what it took.

I hit home and began to hunt. Through Madeline's toy

box. Nothing. Through the sports closet. Soccer balls; a squash ball; two golf balls from who knew where; a moth-eaten old tennis ball. But I needed things the same size and weight. To my bedroom closet. A shoebox full of clean socks Mum had rolled up neatly in pairs. Experimentally, I tossed one up in the air and caught it. Hmmm. A bit light, but they might have to do.

I wandered into the kitchen with Madeline trundling after me, in search of inspiration and an afternoon snack. On my way past the fruit bowl, I absentmindedly fished out the last mandarin orange. Tossed it from one hand to the other, up in the air, in a curving arc. It returned to my hand with a satisfying *thunk*.

Madeline sat on the floor watching me, eyes wide. "Me dat," she said.

I gave her a grin. "Yes, Madeline," I told her. "*Yes!*" Crossing over to the shopping list on the fridge, I wrote *Mandarins*.

I sat down at the kitchen table with Madeline on my lap and peeled the last orange, and we shared it, piece by piece.

THREE-CAR FAMILY

Dad's a milkman. Well, he's not *really* a milkman—not deep down inside, where it counts. Saying he's a milkman, that's like saying . . . that I'm a chef, or a soccer player. Sure, I cook—because I have to. And sure, I play soccer.

And Dad *works* as a milkman. But deep down, he's still what he used to be, before his accident. A fireman. Maybe that's part of the problem.

There's this song that came on the radio once. You know how with some songs, you hear them a million times and you still can't whistle the tune or remember the words, even if your life depended on it? Well, this one was different. Even though I only heard it that once, on the station Mum listens to in the morning when she's making our school lunches, I remember it was about someone's old man being a garbage man and wearing a garbage man's hat and "gorblimey trousers," whatever they are.

Something like that, anyhow. And when I heard it—two years ago, maybe—I had this weird half-memory, half-dream.

Dad dancing around the living room—our old living room, where we lived before—Dad *waltzing* around with me in his arms, singing that song to me, with Mum laughing up at him. Except he was singing: *"My old man's a fireman."*

That's how things used to be, before. Then Dad had his accident, and couldn't be a fireman anymore. Not with his leg the way it was.

We bought a new house with the insurance money and moved straight in. When I remember that time, I remember it as always being night. Night, with Mum and Dad huddled on either side of the kitchen table scribbling on pads of paper, and Dad punching in sums on the calculator with his clumsy, blunt fingers. Night, and Mum and Dad disappearing behind the closed bedroom door to change the dressings on Dad's leg. Night, with long discussions in low voices that stopped if Nick or I came into the room. Night, and Dad with a fresh beer at his elbow and an empty on the floor beside him, and Mum very quiet, with dark smudges under her eyes.

Then suddenly it was morning, and we were all at the breakfast table. Dad was telling us how he and Mum had been looking into a new business opportunity—a new beginning. A thing called a "franchise," that would mean he was his own boss and answered to no one, giving him freedom and independence and making us all rich.

It was a MooZical Milk franchise, and it came with its own territory and established clients and—wait for it!—a special refrigerated milk truck that played a tune and mooed like a cow when you pressed a red button. I thought it was the coolest thing I'd ever heard.

Mum and Dad sank what was left of the insurance money and all their savings into MooZical Milk. There was no risk—it was a watertight license to print money, and Dad couldn't understand why everyone didn't do it. The papers were all signed and the money paid over. We had a special celebration dinner with real champagne, and Nick and I were allowed a tiny glass to drink a toast to "our family's new venture." The milk truck arrived, and it was cooler than cool. We went with Dad on his first run, taking turns to press the button. Even with the limp, Dad seemed like his old self again.

And then, almost overnight, the whole thing turned sour.

Down at the bottom of the hill a brand new shopping complex sprang up, complete with a massive supermarket. Suddenly it was the easiest thing in the world for people to pick up a liter of milk when they did their shopping, or on their way home from work. People left Dad's milk run like rats deserting a sinking ship.

But Dad couldn't go anywhere. He was trapped. All he could do was try his best to make it work. And that's what we'd been doing ever since.

A while back, Dad decided there was no point in trailing out to do deliveries every day. It just used up gas, and time. Gas that cost precious money, and time that could be spent scouring the papers for jobs, sending away applications, and even—some-times—going for the occasional interview. But it seemed there weren't many jobs for an ex-fireman with a limp and a milk run around his neck like a millstone.

So these days, we just did the deliveries on Sundays, Mondays, Wednesdays, and Fridays. People—the ones who still bought their milk from us—just ordered a bit more, to tide them over on the days in between.

The MooZical Milk people didn't think to tell Dad, when he put on his suit and went off to that first meeting with his bad leg dragging behind him, that you need to be fit to be a milkman. Especially if your milk run has long driveways on a steep hill. Up and down the driveways. In and out of the truck, maneuvering your stiff leg like a lump of wood. That didn't seem to occur to them in the interview—or any time after, right up until the papers were signed. And then, even if it had, it would have been too late.

At first, Dad paid a local kid to help with the deliveries. There was no other option. Mum couldn't do it—she had to stay at home and look after us. As soon as he was old enough, Nick helped. I was green with envy. Helping Dad with his milk run—how cool was that?

Then Nick was old enough for a paper route, and I was the one who got to help Dad. And it turned out to be a lot less fun that I'd thought.

Being winter, it was almost dark by the time we started, and cold. A fine drizzle was falling as Dad reversed out of the driveway and into Contour Terrace, and turned to head on up to the top of the hill.

A heavy, brooding silence filled the truck. Dad's knuckles on the steering wheel were white; his eyes glinted under his heavy brows. The wrinkles around his eyes were deep and straight, like cuts. I sat in the passenger seat, small and silent in my rain jacket, making the most of the warmth while it lasted. Talking to Dad in this mood would get a grunt at best. With luck, he'd thaw on the way down the hill.

I used to think it was just because Dad's leg hurt when he was doing the milk run. It took me a long while to realize how much he hated it. He saw it as a kind of failure, I guess—and Dad's a man who hates to fail. He's said it to us often enough: "If you can't succeed at something, don't do it. It's that simple. Black and white, boys—and nothing in between." Sometimes Mum would argue that life was like a photograph—black and white, sure, but with shades of gray giving it meaning and depth. Mum's big on compromise, and on how trying matters more than succeeding. "To you, maybe," Dad would growl, "but not to me."

We headed down from the top of the hill, winding our way along the terraces. Start-stop-start, me hanging on the back like a barnacle; hopping off to collect the empty bottles and put out the full ones; running up and down the drive-ways with rain blowing in my face and trickling down my neck. Dad drove straight past two of our regulars. One was the Sheffields. They had five kids all younger than Nick—I knew two of them from school. They were practically our best customers. I knew not to say anything, though—when

Dad drove past a customer with that look on his face, it meant one thing. Canceled.

At the bottom of the hill, we headed for the home stretch. Down the long avenue I rode along every day to school; left at the traffic lights; start-stop-start. Moo. *Moooo*.

At last, we came to the farthest point of the run— Ballinger Park, where I had soccer practice on Thursdays. Dad turned the truck, and waited for me to shake myself off and jump in beside him. He gave me a little sideways glimmer of a glance, and touched my knee. "Good job, Son." It was his way of saying . . . who knew what, with Dad? But it warmed me from the end of my nose to the tips of my toes.

The traffic light at the intersection was red. Dad shifted in his seat. Rain always made his leg ache, though he wouldn't admit it. Across the road, the huge new indoor sports center loomed up out of the dark. "Must be just about finished." Dad grunted. He put the truck in gear and pulled away, turning into the traffic. I craned my neck back to see.

It was going to be awesome. Just over a year ago, that same block had been covered by derelict old houses. Then they'd been bought up for redevelopment. *Bor-ing*, I'd thought. But then a bulldozer came in and smashed the whole lot down. I spent over an hour watching one afternoon on my way home from soccer. Suddenly it all started to look more interesting.

Next they'd put up a high fence, and cordoned the whole area off with this official-looking red and white tape. Big notices went up. Most said: "No admittance—authorized contractors only." But there was a huge sign right up at the entrance where the trucks went in and out, and it said: "Site of Ignatius Loon Indoor Sports Stadium."

Nick couldn't talk about anything else for weeks. The local papers were full of it—how this old guy, Ignatius Loon, had left a fortune in his will to have it built. Seems he'd lived his entire life in a wheelchair and wanted the local community to have all the opportunities he'd missed out on. Way cool, in a way—but kind of sad, when you think he didn't have a family or anyone to leave all that money to . . . only a whole bunch of people he'd never even met.

It wasn't five minutes before everyone stopped calling it the Ignatius Loon Indoor Sports Stadium—who has the time to say all that? Instead, it became the Igloo—to us kids, to the papers . . . to the whole neighborhood. And it looked like a giant igloo—massive and circular, made out of these huge hexagonal white panels, with a domed top you could see from our house, way up the hill.

But the papers soon ran out of things to say. The old guy must have had a sense of humor, because he'd decided no one was allowed to know what was going to be inside the Igloo until it opened. You could just imagine him up there in heaven, out of his wheelchair and spry as you like, capering around rubbing his hands with glee at the sight of all us kids peering in through the fence, eaten up with curiosity and dying for the great day to arrive.

And now it was nearly time.

The Igloo reared up in all its glory. It was surrounded by

a tarred parking area the size of a football field, almost complete. The huge double doors were firmly shut, as always. Until today, the big electronic billboard out front had been dark and silent, just waiting to light up with who knew what.

I nearly dislocated my neck and yipped so loud Dad practically crashed the truck. Because now, for the first time, a bright red message spilled out into the rain, flashing on and off like the lights on a Christmas tree:

GRAND OPENING: FIVE DAYS TO GO!

CROUP

It rained on and off for the next couple of days.

I rode to school in the rain, and home again in the rain. We weren't allowed outside at break time; instead, everyone mooched around the classroom, and read, and fidgeted, and played tic-tac-toe in the condensation on the windows. And talked, endlessly, about the Igloo and the Grand Opening on Saturday night.

Wednesday morning, everyone woke up in a grump. Dad, because his leg was aching in the constant rain; Nick, because all his sports practices had been canceled and he had cabin fever; me, because bad tempers are catching, and my favorite breakfast cereal was finished. I also had that raw, scratchy feeling at the back of my throat that means you're getting a cold.

Even Madeline was cross, and her nose was running. Mum had made her favorite breakfast: a boiled egg scooped out of the shell, mixed up in her bunny mug with little squares of bread. Totally gross, but Madeline loved it.

But: "Eggy go way!" she said crossly, pushed the mug off her table, and started to cry. If I hadn't caught the mug, it would've smashed for sure. As it was, the eggy, bready goo fell out all over the floor.

"Yuck," said Nick.

Still clutching the mug in one hand, I sneezed—one of those rip-snorting sneezes you don't even feel coming that just about blow the top of your head off.

"Yeeeuuuck!" said Nick.

"Cover your nose and mouth when you sneeze," growled Dad.

Mum looked worried. "I hope you're not getting a cold, Pip. You know what colds are like with you." I did—every single cold I'd ever had ended up giving me croup—and that's nobody's idea of fun, believe me. "I'll make sure I get those mandarins you asked for at the shops today. They're cheap at the moment, and we could all do with some extra vitamin C—it's that time of year, I guess."

She wiped the floor clean and lifted Madeline out of her chair. Madeline kicked her feet and wriggled to get down, then crawled away into the corner and sat there grizzling.

"Hey, Mum," said Nick, tipping back on his chair, "Daniel's niece is only a year old, and she's already walking. She was at soccer practice last week, running 'round every-where. Shouldn't Madeline be walking by now? Heck, she's—what?—eighteen months old!"

Instantly, Dad was on the alert. "She's more than eighteen months. Is that right, Trish? When do babies start to walk?"

Mum's smile looked tired. "It varies, Jim—everyone's different. She'll walk when she's ready. Look how well she's talking—and stringing words together."

My heart was lurching in my chest, like a stone rolling over and over. "I think she's smart not to walk," I said. "Why go to all the trouble of learning to walk when you're the world's best crawler? I reckon Madeline's got it right. I bet she'll still be crawling when she goes to high school. Heck, she'll probably win the Crawling Olympics!" I meant to make them laugh, and most of all, to deflect Dad. But to my horror I saw tears in Mum's eyes. She turned quickly away and started to iron.

"How old was Nick when he first walked? Trish?"

"Oh, Jim . . . I really can't remember."

"Well, I can. I remember him running 'round the garden pushing that red wheelbarrow on his first birthday. He must have been walking long before that."

"Like I said, Jim . . . everyone's different."

"And Pip—what about Pip? How old was he?"

Mum's mouth was set in a tight line. She didn't look at Dad when she answered him. *"I don't remember."*

"He was way older than me," piped up Nick. "Gran said you were worried and took him to a specialist and everything."

Mum's eyes glittered ominously. It wasn't often Mum lost her cool; but when she did, it was best to duck for cover. Even Dad knew that.

"Pip was my second baby. I was too young and inexperienced to realize how different children are . . . how different they should be!"

"So, how old *was* Pip?" Dad persisted.

Mum slammed down the iron, flicked the power off, and yanked out the plug. "Oh, for heaven's sake! Will you let it drop? Nick walked at ten months, Pip at seventeen months. Yes, I *was* worried. Yes, I *did* take him to a specialist. And the specialist told me children reach their milestones at different ages. Like Nick, Pip, and now Madeline. Satisfied?"

Mum picked up her pile of ironing and left the room, slamming the door. "Mummy go bye-bye," said Madeline, and began to cry. The rest of us sat around the table, silence hanging over us like a cloud. Dad's eyes flicked from me to Nick, and back again. With a heavy sigh, he scraped his chair back and lumbered to his feet. I could read his mind like a book.

Nick walked at ten months, Pip at seventeen months. Look at Nick now . . . and look at Pip. And here's Madeline, not even close to walking, and more than eighteen months old! He looked over at her, eyes narrowed. Then, without saying a word, he slowly shook his head and went out, banging the door behind him.

When I arrived home from school, there they were: a dozen shiny orange mandarins, arranged in the fruit bowl with a bunch of bananas and a couple of apples.

My fingers itched. But Nick was sprawled on the sofa eating a peanut-butter sandwich and talking on the phone— to a girl, it sounded like—so I played it cool. Wandered over to the fridge and had a look inside. Yes! Jelly Wobbles! I chose a pineapple one, peeled off the lid, and settled down at the table to eat it, atom by atom.

At long last, Nick finished and slouched out. Quick as a flash I was over at the fruit bowl, grabbed two mandarins, and snuck away to my room. Closed the door behind me. Held a mandarin in each hand. Right! Now what? I remembered what Michael had done, tossing one up, then kind of sliding the other across. It hadn't looked right to me; hadn't been that impressive, to tell the truth. I thought of Mrs. Holland, with those five juggling balls curving through the air. She'd made it look so easy. But somehow I had a feeling it wasn't going to be.

I was right. By the end of half an hour, I was just about ready to give up. I must have dropped those mandarins a million times. Mrs. Holland had looked relaxed, but I felt awkward and stiff; I had a pain like a knife down the back of my neck, and my eyes were watering. And I wasn't even doing it as well as Michael. *Never mind*, I told myself. *Mrs. Holland said it took patience and determination. When you make up your mind to do something, you have to stick to it.*

I didn't feel like eating the mandarins. I never wanted to see another mandarin. I took them to the kitchen and smuggled them back into the fruit bowl. Madeline watched me solemnly from the floor, her little nose running, her eyes like saucers. I scooped her up and wiped her nose gently with a soft tissue. "Juggling, Madeline," I whispered. "Our secret, huh? Don't tell anyone, okay?" She wasn't about to, that was for sure. Not Madeline.

I helped Dad with the milk run that evening, same as usual. Mum offered to do it instead, because of my cold—my nose was streaming, and my eyes felt watery and blurred. But: "Don't pamper the boy, Trish," growled Dad; so off we went. It seemed to take forever.

Dinner was sausages and mash, with peas and corn and a great jug of steaming gravy. I'd looked forward to it all the time we'd been out, but I had a couple of bites, and then didn't want any more.

Mum ran me a hot bath like she used to when I was small, and I headed off to bed way earlier than usual. I drifted in and out of a light doze. Irritating, circular dreams repeated through my mind, and I tossed and turned to try to get away from them. At last, close to midnight, I felt myself slip into a deeper sleep.

I jolted awake to the sound of my own coughing—a harsh, barking sound like a seal. I struggled to sit up and catch my breath. My throat felt closed, as if my windpipe had narrowed to the width of a pinhead. Familiar, sick panic washed through me. Sitting in the dark, shoulders hunched, I fought to breathe. A cough caught at the back of my throat, but I was scared to let it come—scared I wouldn't be able to get my breath back.

Shivering, I slid out of bed and crept down the dark passage to Mum and Dad's room. As quietly as I could, I turned the handle and opened the door a crack. I could see their dark shapes under the blankets and hear Dad's soft, rhythmic snore.

I tiptoed silently to Mum's side of the bed and bent over her. "Pip? Is that you?" She sounded wide awake. No matter how quiet I was, some sixth sense always seemed to let her know I was there.

We padded through to the bathroom, Mum in her dressing gown, me in my pajamas. Mum turned the shower on hot and poured me a plastic cup of cold water from the hand basin. I took it in my shaking hands and sipped.

We sat on the floor, leaning back against the bath. Mum's hair was rumpled, and her face had a crease mark on one side, where she'd been lying. Her eyes smiled at me. "That's it, sweetheart. Just take it a breath at a time. In and out . . . in and out."

She took my hand and held it, rubbing the back gently with her thumb. As I concentrated on breathing, the bathroom filled with steam. Gradually, my breathing eased. I felt the panic drain away; my body relaxed and my eyelids drooped.

Then Mum's hand was on my shoulder. "Bed."

I stumbled to my feet and followed her through the swirling steam. "You'd better come in with me. Then I can keep an eye on you." I nodded. I was too tired to argue; and anyhow, it was what I'd always done, since I was tiny.

Mum groped in the dark for Dad's shoulder, and gave it a shake. "Jim. Jim!"

Dad made a startled, spluttering sound, and sat bolt upright. "Huh? Wazzamarra?"

"It's Pip, Jim. Croup."

Muttering and grumbling, Dad headed for my room, his pillow under one arm. I snuggled down in the hollow where he'd been, breathing in his Dad-smell, cradled by his warmth. Mum slipped in beside me.

"Okay now?"

"Yeah, okay," I croaked. And I knew I would be—the croup never dared come into the sanctuary of Mum and Dad's bed. I felt warm and sleepy and utterly safe, as if I were a little boy again.

A thought floated to the surface of my mind. "Mum," I whispered. "Mum—you and Dad . . . you're so . . . different . . ."

Mum's voice came softly through the dark. "Not as different as you might think, Pippin." I could sense her searching for the real meaning behind what I'd said, the way Mum does. "And you know, sweetheart—just because you're different from someone, it doesn't mean you love them any less. But sometimes it does mean the love is . . . more . . . painful."

I thought of her and Dad . . . of me and Dad. I thought of Madeline, and the look in Dad's eyes that morning.

I wanted to protect her from that look; from the pressure of Dad's expectations and the weight of his disappointment. But I didn't know how. And then suddenly it came to me. It wouldn't work forever; but it would do for now. Someone else could win the Crawling Olympics. My little sister had to walk soon, just like other babies her age. And it wouldn't be hard for her, because she'd have me helping—every step of the way.

I'd learn to juggle, and Madeline would learn to walk. We'd do it together.

TRAINING

We had our first training session the next afternoon, straight after school.

"No time for afternoon snack. Work first, play later. If you're a good girl and try your best, you can have a raisin. Okay?"

With Madeline on my hip, a miniature box of raisins in one hand, and two mandarins in the other, I headed off to my room. Shut the door. Put the mandarins on the bed and Madeline in the middle of the floor. I kept the box of raisins in my hand.

"Now," I explained, "the first thing you have to do is stand up. Like this." I held her under her arms and lifted her gently so she was the right distance from the floor. Her fat little legs in their bright pink leggings stiffened and pushed. She jounced up and down. "Uppy! Uppy! Uppy!" she shouted.

"Yeah, uppy," I told her, hanging on tight so she wouldn't fall over. "But you have to do it yourself. You have to *stand*, see. And once you're standing, then you have to move your legs, one at a time. And that's walking."

She listened solemnly, her eyes very big and dark in her round face. I was sure she understood. I took out a raisin and positioned it carefully on the floor, about three Madeline-steps away from where she was sitting. That would be far enough, the first time.

Instantly, she rocked forward onto all fours and raced across the floor. Picked the raisin up, and popped it into her mouth. Gave me her special zillion-watt smile. "More daisin!" she said happily, holding out her hand.

In the end, that was pretty much as far as we got, that first lesson. But I figured we were off to a good start.

Which was more than could be said for the juggling. I wasn't like Madeline, with my own personal trainer. But like her, I needed help—and I knew just the place to find it. So at break that morning, even though the rain had finally stopped and there'd been a general stampede outside, I had headed off to the school library.

It hadn't been long before I'd found a picture book called *Juggling for Beginners*, with a little kid in a clown costume on the cover. The kid was way smaller than me. If he could do it, so could I!

Now I turned to the first page. *Why learn to juggle?* it said. "Listen to this," I read to Madeline, "*Juggling is something nearly everyone can be good at. In juggling, there are no losers—everyone is a winner! Juggling will help you feel calm and relaxed. It is a great way to set and achieve simple, realistic goals, and forget about all your worries."* Madeline popped a thoughtful raisin into her mouth. She looked dubious. Not me, though—I was on fire. I turned the page. "It says practicing with one ball is the best way to start. You have to learn to make figure-eight patterns with one ball before you move on to two. Looks like I was trying to run before I could walk—or walk before I could crawl."

The book was right—by the end of my session I was feeling much more confident. Okay, I was using only one ball—but I figured next time I'd be ready to try with two.

Once I'd finished practicing, I ate the mandarins. The one I'd been throwing around was pretty squishy, but the other one was okay. Madeline didn't want any—she was full of raisins.

It was Thursday, which meant soccer practice at half past four. I threw on my gear and headed to the kitchen to fill my water bottle. On the way past the fridge, I had a sudden thought. I rummaged around for a pen that worked—no mean feat in our house—and wrote on the list: *raisins*.

When I arrived at practice, the whole team was buzzing. This Saturday we'd be playing the Condors—a really tough team, top of the league. But that wasn't the big news. The really big news was that the selector for the regional squads was coming to watch the game. "He'll be on the lookout for players with that special something," our coach, Andy, told us, trying to sound laidback. "With the Condors doing so well this season, he's probably got his eye on a few of their players. But there are a couple of you who'll interest him, too, I'm sure. Just play your usual game, do your best, and who knows? It could be the start of something exciting. And the best time to practice those skills is right now—so let's get moving!"

All I could think, as I dribbled the ball in and out of the cones, was: *Thank God it's Mum's turn to take me to soccer!* Dad would be safely on the other side of town watching Nick's match; I'd be going with Mum and Madeline in Rubber Band. Mum would do what she always did: spend the entire match talking to the other parents; at the end of it, she probably wouldn't even know the score.

And that suited me just fine.

After practice I changed out of my muddy cleats into my sneakers, hopped onto my bike, and headed home. It was that funny twilight time of day—not quite evening, but dark enough for some of the cars to have their headlights on. The electronic billboard outside the Igloo flashed red in the gray light:

GRAND OPENING: TWO DAYS TO GO!

I freewheeled to a stop and stood there, straddling my bike and staring in through the gate. Two days to go! Heck, it was huge—what could possibly be inside? People were saying all kinds of things: a massive indoor ice rink; a basketball stadium; an entire indoor athletics track; squash courts; a mini-golf course—the theories were getting wilder and more extravagant as the opening grew closer.

I'd been staring in for a couple of minutes before it suddenly hit me: the gate was open. Wide open! The parking area was finished, and there was one lonely vehicle parked way over to the side—a battered, rusty blue jeep, a kind of cross between Rubber Band and Dad's truck.

With an automatic glance over my shoulder to check that no one was watching, I scooted cautiously in through the gate and rode slowly across the huge expanse toward the main entrance. My heart was hammering, and I had a queasy, nervous feeling, as if I were doing something wrong. I knew I wasn't—after all, the gate was open. But still . . .

I stopped at the edge of the paved area in front of the main entrance and stared at the big double doors. Shut tight, same as always. From close up, they were even huger than I'd thought.

And there were still two whole days to wait! In two days the doors would be wide open, and everyone would know what was inside. But for now, I might have been the only person on the planet. Apart from the jeep, the parking lot was empty—it was all mine!

I rode around for a while—doing wheelies; making enormous, swooping circles and speedway turns; jumping my bike over the low concrete curbs. Pretty soon I'd forgotten my nervousness. This was fun! This was cool! I'd tell Katie and Michael tomorrow at school how I'd ridden my bike around the Igloo parking area before anyone else had even been inside, and they'd be green with envy.

I skidded my bike to a stop in front of the blue jeep. The

back was full of all kinds of clutter—ropes, metal clips, and a jumble of harnesses that looked as if they might have something to do with horses. Hey! Maybe there'd be an indoor rodeo!

And it was only then, as I glanced at the Igloo one last time before heading off home, that I noticed it. A small door set back into a kind of porch . . . open just a crack. With light shining through. *Wicked!*

Without hesitating, I slid off my bike and leaned it up against the wall. I touched the surface gently with my fingers. From a distance, the panels looked white and smooth, like blocks of snow; but now that I was right up close, I could see they were pale gray concrete, cool and slightly rough to the touch.

I looked at the slit of light, pretending to decide. But the truth was, there was no decision to make.

With my heart pounding, I crept closer, eased the door open a fraction wider and snuck inside.

INSIDE THE IGLOO

I was in a narrow concrete passageway, which I guessed must be some kind of service entrance, lit by a single electric light bulb. Up ahead—maybe five meters—was another door, also slightly ajar.

I crept up to it. My feet didn't make a sound on the bare concrete floor. I expected any second to hear an irate voice yelling: "You there! *Stop right now!*" But there was nothing—only silence.

I inched the second door open, eased through, and stood there, staring.

I was in a colossal amphitheater dominated by four enormous rectangular sports courts. Each court was enclosed by close-knit green netting: front, back, sides . . . even the top. Wide open galleries ran between the courts, with grandstands three tiers high, where spectators could watch whatever was happening inside those courts.

But what would it be?

I double-checked that there was no one in sight. The

whole place seemed completely deserted. What little light there was came from wall-mounted lamps positioned at intervals around the perimeter. In that huge space, they barely took the edge off the darkness; they were little islands of brightness in the vast gloom. No one could play sports in this! Glancing up, I saw there were powerful overhead fluorescent units suspended from the ceiling. The lights that were on now were probably a low-energy system that kicked in after hours for maintenance people and security.

I edged closer to one of the courts and peered through, hooking my fingers through the net. It gave under the pressure of my hands, stretching as if it were made of some kind of stiff elastic. Far out! With a huge grin, I let myself fall forward onto the springy green net. It gently bounced me back upright again. And again . . . and again. It was like a giant vertical trampoline! Looking through it, I could see cricket wickets . . . basketball hoops . . . even a soccer goal, complete with nets, at each end. How wicked was *that*? The stretchy netting must be so you could play sports—full-on action indoor sports—without the ball flying out and hitting the spectators. But how the heck did you get in there in the first place?

I skirted the wall, hunting for some kind of entrance, my brain going into overload as I absorbed detail after mind-boggling detail.

Over in one corner was an "Action Café," which I guessed would sell fizzy drinks and chips and ice creams and other cool stuff. Next to it was a doorway with a sign:

Tumbletots Adventure Center. Way to go, Madeline!

As I moved farther from the door, it seemed to get darker. There was something spooky about moving stealthily through the gigantic, dimly lit stadium; for a moment, I wondered whether maybe I should sneak out again . . . before someone saw me.

But then, just up ahead, I noticed a stairway; and next to it, a signboard. It was in deep shadow, impossible to read from where I was standing. Moving closer, I saw an arrow pointing up the stairs. The board said:

First Floor
- *Gymnasium and Fitness Center*
- *Saunas*
- *Sunbeds*
- *Action Bowling Alley*

I grinned. Action bowling alley? This was all way, way better than any of us had imagined.

Second Floor
- *Swim Center*
- *Locker Rooms*
- *Administration*

Wait till I told Katie and Michael about this! They'd never believe me!

There was a chain looped loosely across the stairway, at about waist height. I could easily slip under it. In fact, my hand was already reaching for it when I reconsidered. It looked pretty dark up there. It would be way creepy; and what if whoever was in here decided to leave, and locked me in?

Whoever was in here! Whoever—*wherever*. I'd pushed my luck far enough. I'd better go now, while the going was good. But first, I'd complete my circuit of the ground floor. By now, I was over on the opposite side from the door I'd come in through. I might as well head back along the wall I hadn't explored yet.

Halfway back to the entrance, I saw a new doorway I hadn't noticed before. Another sign, like a skeleton of words waiting for the flick of an unseen switch to bring it to life: *Climbing Center*.

Climbing Center? What the heck was a climbing center? I thought of the gym at school, with wooden racks like ladders going up one wall. Maybe it was like that. I was nearly back at the entrance—surely I had time for one quick peek?

I eased the door open onto a passageway similar to the one I'd come in through. But this one had a tough green carpet, and the walls were painted—a bit of window-dressing for the customers, I thought with a grin. Other doorways led off to the left and right. *Isolation Room. Storeroom. First Aid. Bouldering Room.* I tried each one, but they were locked.

Up ahead, the open mouth of the passageway led to a deeper gloom. Even before I reached it, I had an impression of space, openness, and height.

But what I saw when I reached the entrance stopped me dead in my tracks. Suddenly it all made sense. Climbing.
Climbing!

In the strange, unreal twilight, huge walls stretched up into the darkness. I walked softly into the center of the room and turned full circle, staring up, my mind whirling. From here, I could see the room was filled with looped ropes of every color imaginable, suspended by some kind of pulley system.

But the walls—the walls fascinated me. On the outer perimeter, opposite where I'd come in—the curved shell of the Igloo—they sloped inward. In some places, it was a gradual smooth curve; in others, there were shelves and angles and buttresses, like you'd see on a cliff face. On this side, the walls had been painted in smudged shades of brown and beige, like the granite cliffs up in the hills.

And on every other side—everywhere I looked—walls stretched up into the darkness. In some places, they were sheer and vertical, disappearing into the shadows where presumably some kind of roof lay way, way above. The inner wall was far higher than the ceiling of the main sports arena, I realized—it was at least twice as tall, and just looking up at it gave me a spinning sense of vertigo.

In other places, the walls had overhangs, horizontal planes . . . even concave lips. There was one section where two parallel walls reared up side by side, with a narrow crack in between. Would someone—*could* someone—climb up there?

Some of the walls were painted in awesome patterns of orange, yellow, and gray, like a range of mountains disappearing into a distant sunset. In other places they were a dark blue. One wall was covered in cool graffiti-type pictures of lizards and spiders and cartoon creepy-crawlies.

Moving closer, I saw the walls weren't smooth. All over every single wall were tiny holes, like the acoustic tiles in the school auditorium. And screwed into some of the holes, at irregular intervals, were handholds: hundreds and thousands of little lumps and bumps and toggles, every shape and size you could imagine.

I crossed back over to the door, where the wall was highest. It was a deep midnight blue, and stretched up above me higher than I could see. Stepping closer, I felt the floor shift, and gave a little squeak of fright. I moved my foot, prodding slightly. The floor near the wall was squashy, as if it were padded. In case you fell, I guessed.

Reaching out one hand, I took hold of the nearest bump. It was shaped like a crescent moon, and my hand fitted into it as if it had been made for me, my fingers curling snugly into its hollow top.

Looking up, I could see just where I'd put my other hand, if I were going to climb. Without meaning to, I felt one of my feet kick into the wall. Instantly, it found a foothold, solid as a step.

I looked up again. There was the handhold. I reached for it. Suddenly the wall didn't look steep at all. There was a horizontal red line about twice as high as my head. I'd see if I could climb up to it—just that high. If I couldn't get down, I could always jump—the floor was soft; I wouldn't hurt myself. I started to climb.

And in the unreal twilight of the deserted Igloo, it felt as if someone else had taken over my body . . . and my mind. Suddenly I wasn't Pip McLeod, forever messing up. Pip, Pippin, Piphead, Pipsqueak: battling to be the son Dad wanted, and never even coming close. No—this was a new me, Philip McLeod, who'd been hidden away somewhere deep inside . . . who with each new handhold, was slowly but surely clambering his way out.

Hold followed hold: some deep and reassuring, some smooth and almost impossible to grip, some so tiny I didn't think I'd be able to hang on. But I did. My feet felt for footholds, my legs stretching, flexing, pushing me onward and up . . . and up. Up, in a steady rhythm almost like a dance. Up, past the red line. Way, way past.

Gazing up, my eyes searching for the next hold, and the next, I could see my shadow climbing steadily ahead of me. It looked way bigger than me, and very sure of what it was doing and where it was going. My mind was blank; driven on by a force I didn't question or begin to understand, I climbed.

At long last, I reached what I realized must be the top. I felt the proximity of the ceiling above me; and, dimly in the gloom, I could make out a narrow, indented ledge running just beneath it.

Then, for the first time, I thought about getting down. I swallowed. Suddenly my mouth felt very dry. I realized my fingers were aching and starting to go numb. In that instant, cold sweat popped out all over my body. Slick with sweat, my right hand started to slip. Quickly, I reached up and curled my fingers into the deep lip of the ledge.

And at that moment, the lights went out.

THE MIDNIGHT RUN

For what seemed an eternity, I was in free-fall. In the total blackness, direction didn't exist. Up was down; I was spinning in slow motion, dizzy and weightless, adrenaline surging through my blood in a wave so strong it was like liquid fire. If I hadn't had that one solid, unbreakable handhold, I would have fallen for sure.

As it was, I clung there, some primitive instinct for survival locking my fingers, until the spinning gradually slowed and stopped.

I must have closed my eyes when the lights went out. Opening them again was a monumental effort. When I finally did, it made no difference. I couldn't even see the wall, only millimeters from my face. Dimly, my brain registered that though I couldn't see the wall, I could smell it—a faint smell of plaster and fresh paint. *How strange,* observed my brain, *I've heard that blind people's other senses are extra well-developed, to make up for not being able to see. Now it's like suddenly you've gone blind. How interesting that it's true.*

Poor brain, I thought numbly. *In denial, thinking dumb stuff like that when I'm about to fall.* Already I could feel my left leg beginning to cramp and my fingers starting to weaken. Sooner or later, I'd have to let go. It would be like falling in a nightmare . . . except this wouldn't end in a heart-stopping jerk awake, safe in my own bed. It would end in a bone-crunching, pulverizing impact that would snap my spine like a rotten twig and mash my guts to custard.

Unless . . . unless somehow I could climb down, in the pitch dark. Back the way I'd come.

You have to do it, I told myself harshly. *You've got no choice. You have to let go, and slowly make your way down. If you don't, eventually, you'll fall. And when you fall, you'll die. For real.*

But my hand wouldn't obey my brain. I was paralyzed, clinging onto the ledge and my precarious handholds. Logic said: *climb down before you fall.* But my body said: *no way.* And right now my body was calling the shots.

I wondered if it would hurt.

Somewhere far away, I heard someone whistling. *I know what that is*, said my brain. *It's from* My Fair Lady. *Mum's favorite musical.*

I'm going crazy, I thought. The whistling was coming closer. I clung to the wall, hardly daring to breathe. If I could hear them—whoever they were—they could hear me if I yelled. And then somehow, they would help me. Get me down. Rescue me. Even if I fell, it wouldn't be so bad. At least, I wouldn't fall alone in the dark.

I drew a shallow, shuddering breath. And at that moment, someone came into the room below me. With some extra sense I never knew I had, I felt their silent footfalls on the floor and the vibration of their presence in the air. More importantly, the darkness lightened slightly, though I still couldn't see the wall in front of me.

Flashlight, said my brain.

"Keys, keys, keys," said a cheerful male voice far below. "Where the merry hell are you? I'm late enough already—Chris'll kill me!"

"Help," I croaked.

"Yeeeeaaaaargh!" yelled the man, so loud I nearly let go in fright. There was the jingle and clink of something being dropped.

Keys, said my brain.

"Help me," I whispered. My arms and legs were beginning to shake.

A dim, ghostly circle of light played along the wall until it found me, then wavered and stopped. The silence seemed to go on forever.

Then the voice floated up from below—deep, adult, in control. "Hang on. Hang on tight, while I turn the light on. Be ready for the light, kid, do you hear me? Close your eyes and be ready. And hang on. I'll be back."

Running footsteps. The dark again. I closed my eyes.

Then blinding light against my eyelids, like a blow. I pressed my face against the wall. Breathed in the paint. Footsteps, running, returning. The voice: "Kid . . . you have to climb down."

"I can't. I can't move."

"You have to. I can't come up and get you. *You have to do it yourself.*"

"I can't." My voice was quavering on the edge of tears. "I'm scared. I can't let go. I'm stuck."

"Of course you can let go. You're not stuck, you only think you are. You climbed up; you can climb down. Simple. Take it one step at a time. I'll talk you down. The sooner you do it, the easier it'll be. Just do what I say, right? And whatever you do, don't look down. Come on—you'll be fine. Now, see that red hold just beside your head?" I saw it. "Let go of the top ledge, slow and easy, and take hold of it." It was long and thin, shaped like a lizard. It looked big enough to grip easily. I imagined my hand letting go; reaching for the lizard; holding it, with my fingers dug deep into the sides. I imagined my feet, standing on solid ground again; walking out of there.

I took a deep, slow breath. Let go. Grabbed the lizard. Tight.

"Great, good, well done. Keep moving now, and as you move, you'll loosen up—you'll see. Your left foot—that's the one. There's a hold, down maybe thirty centimeters—you can reach it easily. It's a big foothold, like a step. Better than the one you're on now. Come on, kid. Smooth and easy now; easy does it."

One step at a time, hold by hold, I worked my way down that wall. I don't know if it took a minute . . . ten minutes . . . an hour. But all the way—every step—the man's calm, patient voice talked me down. That whole time, I didn't look down. It felt as if I'd spent my life staring at the dark blue paint with its pattern of tiny holes, groping for handholds with numb fingers and feeling for footholds I couldn't see.

And then I groped with my foot . . . and it touched the floor. *Floor!* yelled my brain. *Floor! Floor! Floor!* But I didn't believe it. My hands still locked on their holds, I looked down to check. It *was* the floor. Instantly, my body turned to putty. I dropped like a stone, landing on my butt on the padded mat. I fell over backward and stared at the ceiling way above me, up the endless wall.

A grim-faced stranger was staring down at me. "What on Earth were you doing up there? What kind of a climber are you—what kind of *idiot* are you—to go up a wall without safety equipment?"

The old brain was still ticking away on autopilot. *Early twenties, maybe? Blue eyes, snapping with angry electric sparks. Unshaven; reddish-blond stubble catching the light like copper wire. Hair to match, untidy, scraped back roughly in a pony tail. A gold earring in one ear. A rugged face with more than a hint of wildness—like a pirate, or a highwayman. And check it out—his hands are shaking!* babbled Brain. *He must have been terrified you'd fall!*

I stumbled stiffly to my feet. "I . . . I'm sorry . . . I really am," I stammered. "Thanks for helping me." I looked down at my feet—miraculously, unbelievably—on solid ground again. "I couldn't have done it without you."

"Damn right you couldn't," he snapped. "If I hadn't

forgotten my keys I'd be far away by now, and you'd be . . . God knows where."

"I'm sorry," I repeated. What else could I say? He was right—I was an idiot.

"What the heck made you do it? Every climber knows the basics—safety first. Rule number one."

"I'm not a climber," I muttered. "I've never climbed before."

"You . . . *you've never climbed before*? You've never climbed before . . . and you made it up the Midnight Run, in bad light—*and down again*?"

"I dunno . . . I guess. You talked me down."

There was a flicker of something other than anger in his eyes. "Well, assuming total ignorance is an excuse, I suppose I'll have to accept that. Though there's a fine line between ignorance and stupidity. But I want an answer before I throw you out. *Why?* What the heck made you pull a stunt like this?"

I felt myself blushing. All of a sudden my knees were trembling; I was scared they'd collapse and dump me in a heap at the angry guy's feet. "I don't know," I mumbled. "I guess . . . I guess it seemed like a good idea at the time."

"It seemed like a good idea at the time," he echoed. "You climbed the Midnight Run without a harness because *it seemed like a good idea*?" His wide mouth, thin-lipped with anger a second before, relaxed into a crooked grin. He threw back his head and started to laugh; and laughed . . . and laughed . . . and laughed. Next thing I knew, I was laughing, too—uncontrollable, hysterical waves of laughter that went on and on as if they'd never stop.

Then we were looking at each other, smiling. "Well, kid, looks like you got away with it. And if you've really never climbed before, maybe you should think about starting. Not many people could do what you've just done, that's for sure. Come along to the Grand Opening on Saturday; see what it's all about." He held out his hand. "I'm Rob Gale. Climbing instructor at the Igloo, and solo member of the after-hours rescue squad! At your service."

I held out my hand, and we shook. I was about to say "I'm Pip," but something stopped me. I looked directly into his blue eyes, and took a deep breath.

"I'm Phil," I told him. "Phil McLeod."

THE SECOND MANDARIN

I was home late. Way late.

Skidding my bike into the driveway in the dark I practically collided with Dad, heading back from the woodpile with the ax.

"Where the hell have you been?" he growled. "I was about to come looking for you—and when I found you, there was going to be trouble. Get inside and under the shower. Make sure you clean your cleats for Saturday. Put that bike away, and bring in some of the logs I've split for the fire. It's your turn to set the table—and what about your homework?" He looked at his watch. "Well, come on, don't just stand there! *Move it*—dinner in five minutes!"

I was used to Dad's barrage of orders. Automatically, my mind sorted them into a tidy stack: bike; logs; shower; table; dinner; cleats; homework.

Fifteen minutes later—Dad's "five minutes" hardly ever matched anyone else's—we were all seated around the kitchen table, watching Mum dish up thick, steaming slabs of macaroni and cheese. I had macaroni and cheese once at Katie's house, but Mrs. Wood didn't make it like Mum. I doubt anyone does—with a layer of sliced leftover sausages, another layer of tomato, and a thick, golden crust of mixed-together breadcrumbs and grated cheese. I suddenly realized how hungry I was. I shoveled up a tottering forkful, and maneuvered it toward my mouth. The steam curled up and tickled my nose.

But Dad had other ideas. "Well? How was soccer practice?'

Reluctantly, I lowered my fork. "Okay," I mumbled. The untold news of the selector's visit sat in the forefront of my mind, rubbing shoulders with images of the Igloo . . . the climbing wall . . . Rob Gale.

I pushed them all away. "Okay," I said again, more firmly. "Good, I guess."

"Anything interesting happen?" asked Dad innocently, around a mouthful of macaroni.

I darted a glance at Nick. Did he know? Had he told? He was piling into his plateful like it was his last meal on Earth, eyes fixed on his plate.

I chewed and swallowed, considering. I knew that look of Dad's. But—"No, nothing much . . ."

"That's not what Murray Wood just spent half an hour telling me over the fence, while I was splitting the kindling."

"What did he tell you, Dad?" asked Nick.

Dad paused for effect, scraping his fork around his plate, then passing it across to Mum for seconds.

"He said Katie told him there's going to be a selector at

your game on Saturday, Pip. Interesting, huh? I thought so. So did he. So did Katie—interesting enough to mention to *her* dad, anyhow."

I felt myself blushing. "Oh—yeah! I forgot . . . Andy did mention something about a selector. But he's just coming to . . . you know . . . kind of have a look, and stuff. It's no big deal."

Dad's eyes glinted shrewdly. Like my brother says, you can fool some of the people some of the time—but it takes Nick to fool Dad.

"Big deal or not, I'm coming to that game. Listen to me, Son. You can spend your life grubbing around in the mud with the no-hopers, or you can get somewhere with your sport—make something of yourself. You have to start somewhere—and Saturday's match could be your big chance." Dad was chomping away on his dinner like a robot, his eyes gleaming in a way I knew all too well—a way I'd come to dread. "It's up to you what you make of your life. I've said that before, and I'll say it again." That was true enough. Dad was constantly saying it; he should've had it tattooed on our foreheads at birth. "It's all down to mental attitude. You've got the skill. It's up to you to make it happen—up to you, and no one else!" He banged his fist on the table, making the tomato-sauce bottle do a little jump in the air and knocking over the pepper grinder.

Madeline was watching him with wide eyes, a wedge of apple clenched in one fat fist.

Nick finished his plateful, and put his knife and fork

together tidily. "Yeah, I've heard about this selector guy," he said casually. "He goes 'round all the teams, like a talent scout. Then the players he picks out go to a special trial, over a couple of weeks. From the guys that try out, the best get picked for the zone team. There's some kind of zone tournament—I'm not sure when—with special training and everything. And based on performances in the zones, they pick the players for the Highlands squads—under fourteens, under fifteens, and junior youth."

We didn't need Nick to tell us that getting onto the Highlands squad was what it was all about. Whatever your sport happened to be—swimming, hockey, basketball, you name it—playing for the Highlands regional team was just about the greatest thing you could hope to achieve. The Highlands soccer squads all had special coaching by top professionals, and got to travel and take part in tournaments and stuff.

More than that, though, there was this kind of aura surrounding Highlands teams that made them every kid's dream from the moment they put on their first pair of shin pads.

And then there was the uniform: this super-cool purple and green—the colors of the mountains, Dad said. Highlands players had team tracksuits, too, in the same purple and green, with *Highlands* across the back.

Whenever you saw a kid in one of those track tops, they'd be walking taller than anyone else. Like royalty. Without them even having to say a word, that track top announced: *I've made it. I've arrived. Envy me—and eat your heart out.*

Mum was talking. "But Jim, isn't it my turn to go to Pip's match this week? And I've promised Joanna Sinclair my recipe for oatmeal pancakes. . . ."

Good try, Mum.

"Write it out and I'll give it to her. You can go next week."

"That'll be great," says Nick. "The week after, Ivan Kingsley—that's the selector—is coming to watch my game." Dad looked up from his plate so fast I thought he'd crick his neck. "He phoned and spoke to me about it today—Ivan Kingsley did," Nick went on into the sudden silence. "Seems our coach's already put forward some names for special consideration. Automatic entry into the zone trials, Ivan says—so for those guys, the game in two weeks is just a formality. Daniel. Tim." He looked down. A modest smile. "And me."

Of course.

The unspoken words hung there above the kitchen table, so clear that I knew if I looked up I'd see them dangling right next to the ceiling light.

Dad gave a small snort of satisfaction. "Good job," he grunted. "Well then, Pip, it's one down, one to go. Imagine that: two McLeod boys at the zone tournament; two McLeod boys playing for Highlands!"

He pushed his chair back, stood up, and helped himself to a piece of Madeline's apple on the way to the door.

I stared down at my macaroni and cheese, congealing on my plate.

Dad's footsteps stopped at the doorway. When he spoke,

his voice was gruff. "I'm proud of you, Son."

I didn't need to look up to know who he was talking to.

That night, the croup came again.

I felt it creep up on me as I lay on my side unable to sleep, staring at the gray glow of moonlight beyond my closed curtains. I was remembering the Midnight Run—not so much remembering it, as reliving it. The wall towering above me . . . the way my hands found the holds as if they belonged there . . . the feeling of recognition, certainty, completion . . . how I'd somehow become one with the climb. But as I lay there, it felt as if the air were growing steadily thicker, from the consistency of nothing . . . to water . . . to oil . . . to syrup . . . to peanut butter . . .

I sat up and coughed, the old familiar seal bark. *Here we go again.* Mum used to say I'd grow out of my croup; that it was a childhood ailment, caused by an immature windpipe. Well, I was still waiting.

I groped for my old sheepskin slippers with the holes in the toes and slid my feet into them. They felt cozy and comforting. I shrugged on my pajama top. These days, the sleeves didn't even cover the bones of my wrists. Then I crept down the dark passage to Mum and Dad's door. With my hand on the doorknob, I hesitated. In my mind's eye I saw Mum's face: pale, lined, drawn, loving . . . and tired.

Madeline had woken after I'd fallen asleep last night, and Mum was worried she might have an ear infection. I had come in to breakfast to find Mum on the sofa with the baby snuggled in her arms, both fast asleep.

Sucking air in, struggling not to cough, I turned away and headed for the kitchen. The blinds were never closed, and the room was washed with moonlight. I poured myself a glass of water and stood sipping it, looking out at the scatter of lights far below. From where I stood, I could see the Igloo. The moonlight reflecting off its dome made it glow just like a fortuneteller's crystal ball. *The Midnight Run . . .*

I sipped again, and coughed. Then I went through to the bathroom, scooping two mandarins out of the fruit bowl on my way past.

I closed the door and stripped off my pajamas. Turned the shower on full, and hopped in. Stood there feeling the hot water cascade soothingly over my bare body as the steam worked its healing way into my lungs, gradually loosening the stranglehold on my throat.

At long last, I dried myself and wrapped my towel around my waist. Unlike the night before, I was wide awake; I could still feel a slight catch when I breathed, telling me it wasn't over yet.

Leaving the shower running—hot water only now—I reached for the oranges. Using the same inward-scooping throw I'd used before, I threw the first orange up in an arc toward the other hand. Just as it was coming down, I threw the second orange up, so they crossed over in the air.

Crossed over—and landed on the bathroom floor.

I picked them up, and tried again. And again. And again.

Focusing on the mandarins, concentrating on my throws and the arcs they made in the air, I felt my shoulders begin to relax. My thoughts cleared. Saturday's soccer match . . . the selector . . . Dad . . . Nick . . . the Igloo and the Midnight Run and Rob Gale . . . all melted away like ghosts in the swirling steam.

Nothing mattered anymore. Nothing except the mandarins, and me.

THE BIG MATCH

"Has anyone seen my socks?"

"Look on the drying rack—they should be there."

"Those are Pip's—they're way too small for me. Pipsqueak! Have you taken my socks?"

"These are mine—I know because of the hole in the heel. And I've already put them on."

Soccer socks are like an ancient instrument of torture—okay when they're new, but wash them once and they shrink into stiff, tight tubes. It's almost impossible to get them up over the bulky shin pads; by the time you eventually manage, you're covered in sweat and more out of breath than after an entire soccer match.

"Let me look. Hey! Those *are* mine! These are yours—they're way smaller! And now I'm going to have to wear socks that've had your smelly feet in them. I'll catch a disgusting disease—foot rot or leprosy or something."

Dad was pacing in the hallway. "Pip! Are you ready? Hurry up, or I'll leave without you!" This was Dad's constant threat—to take us wherever we were going and leave us behind in the process. Yeah, right, Dad!

"Hang on, I'm coming! Has anyone seen my water bottle? Mum, where's my water bottle?"

"Hey, Pipsqueak, where d'you find a dog with no legs?"

"I haven't got time for your stupid jokes! I'm going to be late! Where's my water bottle?"

"*Where you left it!*" honked Nick, collapsing on the sofa with his legs in the air.

"Nick, you'd better start putting those socks on, or we'll be late. Madeline, how did you manage to get porridge in your *hair*?"

At last, we were roaring along the freeway in the truck, Dad scowling with his usual Saturday morning tension, me with the map book open on my lap, trying to figure out the quickest way there.

"Now, Son," Dad was saying, "I want to see some positive, aggressive play. When you tackle, tackle like you mean it. Go in there with a hundred and ten percent commitment. At *least*."

"Yes, Dad."

"And you've got to stop this *cringing* away from the ball, dammit! Go *to* the ball—that's what he'll be looking for. Players who *make* the play, who dictate the flow of the game. Powerful players! Players who get *stuck in*! If you wait for the ball to come to you, you'll wait forever!"

Dad's tirade faded into the background. A scenario was playing itself out in my mind. *The family at the dinner table:*

Madeline in her highchair, Dad carving the roast lamb. We hardly ever had lamb, it was too expensive. I dwelt on the thought for a second, tasting the mint sauce. . . . *And then the phone rings. Dad grumbles about phone calls at dinnertime; Nick hops up to answer it. "Yeah? Yeah! Hi, Ivan, how're ya doing?" He silently mouths to us: "It's Ivan—Ivan Kingsley!" Then into the phone again, grinning: "Hey, Ivan, I . . . huh? Who? You . . . want to speak to Philip? You mean* Pip? *Uh—guh—duh."*

I sit there eating my lamb, cool as a cucumber. Nick passes over the phone to where I sit, like a king, my plate piled high and every eye on me.

"Hi there, Ivan," I say.

"Phil," he says, "good to talk to you. I . . ."

"*Pip!* Are you listening to me?"

"Huh? Uh . . . yes, Dad."

"The most important thing—the *critical* thing!—is to be noticed. On every soccer field, in every game, there are always a couple of players who stand out from the crowd. You have to be one of them. That selector needs to have you right under his nose, doing exciting things with the ball everywhere he looks—things he can't possibly overlook. Things that'll make him sit up and say: *Yes!*"

I wondered what the selector would be like. *Ivan Kingsley.* The name conjured up a picture of a tall, blond, godlike figure with piercing gray eyes that saw everything and missed nothing, especially mistakes. A twinge of queasy nerves tightened in my gut. He'd be wearing . . . what would he be wearing? Selectors and talent scouts were always in disguise, weren't they? He'd be wearing a dark coat, like a spy, and carrying a miniature recorder he'd mutter into when he thought no one was looking.

"And accurate passes—make every pass count! Don't boot the ball into nowhere, that doesn't impress anyone! He'll be looking for vision—vision and skill! First, control the ball. That's the key. Then, look around. You . . ."

An image flashed into my mind. It was me, with my same thin, serious face, but taller and with broader shoulders, standing proud in a Highlands purple and green tracksuit, like I owned the world. And Dad beside me, one arm over my shoulders, beaming at the camera with his best, proudest, crinkliest, whaley smile.

Maybe it was some kind of premonition—a weird wrinkle in time. I hoped so. Because one thing was for sure: I was going to give it my very best shot. I was going to do everything in my power to win those Highlands colors.

I'd do it for Dad.

The truck lurched to a stop. Dad gave me a manly shove on the shoulder that knocked me back against the door, the armrest connecting painfully with my ribs. "Just remember everything I've told you and you'll be fine," he said. "Now get out there and *go for it*."

Lugging my bag, I plodded over to where our team was warming up, keeping an eye out for Ivan Kingsley. There was no sign of him—just our guys, Andy's tall figure in the thick of them, and the Condors over on the other side of the field doing some kind of complicated drill with what looked like a hundred soccer balls.

Katie was kicking a ball up into the air over and over, hopping around on the other foot to keep her balance. "Seventeen, eighteen, nineteen, twenty, twenty-one, twenty-two, twenty-three . . ."

"Hi, Katie."

The ball bounced away across the grass. "Now look what you've made me do! I was on track to beat my record." She glared at me, then relented. "Anyway, hi yourself." She gave me her usual grin. "Ready to knock the socks off the great Ivan the Terrible?"

"If he even comes," I said.

"He's already here."

"What? Where?" I looked wildly around. Was he hiding behind a tree or something?

Katie rolled her eyes. "Over there, Dumbo!"

My mental image of the mysterious skulking Ivan Kingsley vanished like a wisp of smoke in the wind. A dapper little man was deep in conversation with the other team's coach. He was wearing track pants . . . *and a purple and green track top*. I couldn't believe I hadn't noticed him before. He was just so different from what I'd expected! He was short—about my height—with a bald patch and glasses. He looked like a little monk . . . except for that track top. Now I could see he was drawing every eye on the field like a magnet. Everyone kept darting sly glances at him, and then looking away quickly in case he noticed.

The knot in my stomach pulled tighter.

"What d'you reckon he's saying?" I whispered.

"Probably: *See that girl over there? I bet she'd've beaten the world record if that dumb guy hadn't distracted her. Even so, she's a shoo-in for the team!*"

"Right, guys, listen up," barked Andy. I could tell he was trying his best to be cool, but there was an extra urgency about him linked by an invisible thread to the little man in the Highlands top. "We went over everything at practice, and I don't have any more to add. You all know your positions; you all know your jobs. Try to forget Ivan over there." Thirteen pairs of eyes swiveled across the field, and quickly away again. We all looked down and scuffed our cleats. "The Condors are a tough team, and they'll give you a run for your money. Just play your normal game, and do your best. Go out there and have fun. Good luck!"

Standing out on the field waiting for the whistle, I hardly dared look for Dad. Two prayers were repeating in an endless loop in my mind. The first one went: *Please let him notice me; please let me be picked. Please let him notice me; please let me be picked.* The second one went: *Please let him not notice Dad. Please make Dad invisible. Please let him not notice Dad. Please make Dad invisible.*

I snuck a glance over at Dad's usual post, on the opposite side from the rest of the parents. Today, though, the Condors' supporters had stationed themselves there. There was no sign of Dad. For a moment, my heart gave a little skip of hope. Maybe he'd left! Maybe my prayer had been answered, and he'd somehow disappeared, or gone home, or . . .

But no, there he was. Standing away from the main group of parents, with Katie's dad beside him looking uncomfortable. Dad's hands were deep in the pockets of his old green parka, and his shoulders were hunched. For the time being at least, he was still as a statue, and mercifully silent. A short distance away stood the trim figure of Ivan Kingsley, in majestic solitude, with a clipboard in one hand and a pen in the other.

My guts gave one last agonizing twist, the whistle blew, and we were off.

The first half passed in a blur, fast and furious. In spite of what Andy had said, everyone was going all out to play better and harder than ever before—and that applied to the Condors as well.

And were they a strong team! They had this midfielder who was an absolute magician—even Mark, our star player, couldn't get the ball off him. Within the first five minutes he'd scored; two seconds later he was off again, and I thought *Hoo boy, the writing's on the wall—two goals down in the first six minutes; we might as well pack our bags and head home.* But I'd counted out Katie. She went at the midfielder like a charging rhino, and when he tried the nifty footwork that left Mark standing in his wake, Katie stayed right with him, anticipating every move. Then one spindly leg shot out and hooked the ball from between his feet; and while he was floundering around wondering where it had gone, she was off down the field with the ball skipping ahead of her and the Condors' attackers trailing behind.

She ran into more trouble than she could handle just past the halfway mark, though, and I was unguarded on the wing. Back came her foot: *thwack!* Straight to me—and the goal in front of me, like a gift. I gave the ball a kick, chased it, and booted it with all my might straight at the middle of the goal. I put everything I had into that shot.

It hit the goalie's outstretched gloves with a smack that almost knocked him over; he staggered, looking wildly for the ball, which was ricocheting toward the corner post. And suddenly there was Katie again, out of nowhere: *"Pip!"* A classic pass, bouncing once, then arcing right onto the front of my cleat, the laces, the sweet spot right where Dad said you should always kick. The goalie was still blundering around out of his box; the ball crossed behind him, and smacked into the back of the net.

I couldn't believe it! I'd scored! I could hear Dad yelling, "Great goal, Philip McLeod! What a shot, Philip!" Even in my moment of glory, part of me cringed to hear him—it was for the selector's benefit, of course. Dad was as transparent as a two-year-old.

Then the whole team was crowding around Katie and

me, giving us high-fives and slapping us on the back, and Dad's voice was drowned out in the general hullabaloo. We took our positions for the kickoff . . . but not before I'd snuck a peek over at Ivan Kingsley.

Sure enough, his head was down and he was scribbling away. I half expected Dad to be peering over his shoulder checking he'd spelled my name right, but he was next to Mr. Wood, on his best behavior.

It was the match of the season, no doubt about it. By the end of it, the parents on both sides were so hyped up even Dad blended right in.

Andy, who was reffing the second half, was checking his watch; the score was locked at three goals each. We were all dead on our feet, dragging ourselves around the field praying the whistle would blow. For us, it would be a staggering, unbelievable victory just to tie.

Then out of nowhere popped Katie again, ducking and diving between the Condors like a little ferret. Slipped a pass just beyond the reach of their right wing to Mark . . . and he lofted it over the lot of us, into the empty expanse in front of the goal.

We all took off after it, chasing it down like a pack of hounds. The guy marking me was big and husky with a kick like a pile driver, way taller than me; but when it came to speed, I just about had the edge.

We thundered down the field, neck and neck.

Then, with a desperate, diving skid, I threw myself into

the ball; felt my foot connect with something; and was rolling over and over on the ground, dimly aware of a flying shape leaping over me like a hurdler, and the crowd going wild.

Then Katie was dragging me to my feet and hugging me. "You did it! You're a legend! You did it, Piphead! We've won! I could kiss you—almost!" Her muddy face was streaked with sweat and split by a grin like a slice of watermelon.

Triumph surged through me, swamping my exhaustion. I'd scored two goals! I'd scored the goal that won the crunch match against the Condors! Me, Pip McLeod! *And I'd done it right under the selector's nose!*

It had been perfect—way beyond my wildest dreams.

There was just one thing missing. "Almost?" I grinned at Katie; and then her arm was flung roughly around my neck, just about wrenching my head off, and her mouth cannoned into my cheekbone in a resounding smack.

Not exactly romantic. But a kiss, just the same—a kiss from Katie.

I was sitting on the grass taking my cleats off and Katie was devouring one of her disgusting health bars. Dad and Mr. Wood were grunting away about the game in Dad-speak, saying nice things about each other's kid, and carefully avoiding any mention of their own. A figure detached itself from the huddle of the Condors' team and strutted toward us across the field. A trim little figure in a purple and green track top.

I blinked, and checked left and right. There was no one else near. It had to be! He was coming to talk to us! I hopped up, stumbling over my trailing shoelace and nearly landing back on my butt in the mud. Katie froze in mid-chew. The four of us stood staring at Ivan Kingsley approaching across the grass, as if we'd been turned to stone.

KATIE

Dad was striding across to meet him, hand outstretched. "Well, good to meet you, Ivan," he said, in this bluff, hearty voice. "Great game, huh? I'm Jim McLeod, Philip's father; and this here's my son, Philip McLeod—as you obviously know."

There was a strange look on Ivan Kingsley's face as he shook Dad's hand and smiled briefly at me. A look that for a second I couldn't place . . . embarrassed? Then his smile widened, and he looked right past Dad and me, standing there with my hand half held out and my shoelace trailing and my heart banging away like a jackhammer.

"And you must be Mr. Wood, Katie's dad," said Ivan Kingsley, putting one hand on Mr. Wood's shoulder and the other on Katie's. "What a performance you turned in today, young lady! Great ball skills—you're a real provider, a classic utility player—with just the team focus I'm looking for." As he spoke, he was shepherding them both gently away into a select little huddle that excluded Dad and me as surely as if a door had been slammed in our faces.

I felt my cheeks burn and tears sting my eyes. And then, in an awful moment of clarity, I realized what the look had been on Ivan Kingsley's face.

Pity.

Dad ranted all the way home. There was no mention of the Dairy Den.

"I can't believe it! You scored two goals, dammit! And what did Katie do? A couple of halfway decent passes; then swanned around like a bloody ballerina! What the hell is this guy looking for—a pretty face?"

"Katie had a great game," I muttered. "She made that first goal I scored. You even said so to Mr. Wood."

"Well, of course I did! You can't say what you really think, especially to a neighbor. A soccer field's no place for a girl—and the zone trials! Pah! I can't believe it! And he calls himself a selector! I've a good mind to put in an official complaint. . . ."

I tried not to listen, but this time I couldn't shut his words out. By the time we reached the hill, he'd exhausted the subject of Katie—for now, at any rate—and switched to me. "Let's face it, you could have done more. Your passing was sloppy at best . . . and you've never been strong on the ball. Stealing the ball off you is like taking candy from a baby. You have to learn that goals aren't everything. If you want to play top-level soccer, you'll need to change your attitude.

Toughen up. Be hungrier. Now that boy Mark, he's got grit! And your brother: another prime example of the kind of player . . ."

I listened numbly. How I deserved to have been chosen for the trials, and how I didn't. How goals mattered, and how they didn't. How I had to develop the grit that Nick was born with . . . and Katie had by the truckload, without it counting because she was a girl. I couldn't work out whether Dad was defending me or attacking me. Whether he felt I'd done well, or let him down. Was proud, or ashamed. Loved me . . . or wished he had another kind of boy for his son.

Dad slammed into the house and disappeared behind the newspaper in the living room, broadcasting my failure more clearly than if he'd used a megaphone.

I sat on the edge of the porch and undid my other cleat. I'd used these special knots so the laces wouldn't come undone, and it took forever. Then I slipped into the bathroom, avoiding the kitchen with its clatter of dishes, and Mum and Nick's cheerful chatter. I didn't want to see anyone. I didn't want to have to try and explain what had happened. I didn't understand it myself. All I understood was that there was a huge, aching void deep down inside me, and I needed to be on my own until it went away.

I showered and changed into saggy old track pants and a sweatshirt. Went through to my room, and lay on the bed with the door closed and my pillow over my head.

KATIE

After a while, I heard Mum's soft knock. "Pip? Lunch is ready."

"I don't want any," I muttered.

"Pip? Did you hear me?"

"I don't want any lunch!" I yelled.

A long time later, I heard a funny, scratching snuffle near the bottom of my door, followed by a couple of irregular thumps.

I swung my legs off the bed and opened up. In snuffled Madeline, her cold making her sound like a baby bulldog. She reached the middle of the floor, rocked back on her bottom, and held her arms up to me. "Uppy!" she ordered. "Biffin tiss!"

She didn't look her most appetizing. There were smears of chocolate around her mouth, and dried snot crusted over her bright red cheeks like glaze on a bun.

But I picked her up and gave her a kiss, burying my face in her soft baby neck, breathing in her special smell of apple puree, baby powder, and Essence of Madeline. It didn't matter to me that she was dirty and snotty and full of germs. I loved her just the way she was.

Then, on top of everything else, I realized I'd left my math homework at school. It was an algebra sheet we'd been given last thing on Friday. I'd been planning to finish it after lunch, so it would be out of the way by five o'clock, when we needed to leave for the Grand Opening of the Igloo.

Originally, I was going to suggest we all go together—Katie, me, and Michael. But Katie had kissed me . . . and that changed everything. Now I thought maybe just the two of us might go. Just Katie and me.

It was weird, but now, after the business with Ivan Kingsley, I felt kind of shy about talking to Katie. It was as if suddenly there were some kind of barrier between us, charged with electrical energy that was pushing me away.

It's in your mind, I told myself sternly. *You're just jealous. You'd be crazy to let this come between you. Especially now, when Katie's finally starting to see you as more than just a friend. Go on over; congratulate her; ask what Ivan Kingsley said. She must be dying to tell you. Do it, no matter how much it hurts. Borrow the homework sheet. Ask her to the opening. Remember the kiss! What's more important—a lousy soccer trial, or a real-life kiss from the girl of your dreams?*

I slipped out of the house and over to the gap in the hedge. We used to sit there for hours when we were younger, but we didn't do that now. Instead, we'd walk to the park and swing on the swings and talk; or catch the bus to the mall and cruise the shops, outdoing each other with the crazy things we'd buy if we were millionaires.

These days, we mostly used the phone to talk or arrange to meet up. But occasionally we still used our old secret signal at the fence; and today, it somehow felt right. I squatted down and whistled: the drawn-out descending single note that was supposed to sound like a starling, that we'd been so proud of perfecting when we were little. I listened for the answering call that meant Katie was coming. Whistled again . . . and again.

Nothing.

My heart sank another notch. *You're not a kid anymore! Use the phone.*

I went into the deserted kitchen and dialed Katie's number. The phone rang for ages before Mrs. Wood answered it. "Hi, Mrs. Wood; it's me, Pip. Can I speak to Katie?"

"Of course, dear. Hold on, I think she might still be in the . . . no, she's right here; I'll put her on."

Murmured voices. Then Katie: "Hi."

"Hi, Katie." Even to me, my voice sounded different—kind of forced and cheerful. "Well done on the trials. Way to go."

"Thanks. You played well, too. It was your goal that won the game. Down with the Condors! Colts forever!"

"Down with the Condors! Colts forever!" I echoed, back on familiar ground. "Hey, Katie—I was wondering . . . that math sheet. Can I borrow it?"

"Sure."

"Great!" I was feeling more cheerful. "I'm on my way over. See ya!"

"I . . ."

Katie's voice came faintly down the line just as I went to slam down the receiver. I picked it up again: "What? Katie?" But she was gone.

I scooted down our drive and up Katie's, then jumped up the steps to her porch, a mirror image of ours, and just as familiar. Rang the bell, and heard its cheerful *bing-bong* echo through the house.

Mrs. Wood opened the door. She was holding the math sheet and looked flustered. "Here you are, dear. Katie's just . . ."

"Just what?" I knew she was there; I'd talked to her a minute ago.

Katie's voice drifted out from the depths of the house. "Oh, let him in, Mum—it's only Pip! I'm perfectly decent!"

Mrs. Wood gave me the homework sheet, along with a funny look I didn't understand. I headed for Katie's room, where I tapped on the door and popped my head 'round.

Katie was at her dressing table drying her hair, wearing a sky-blue dressing gown thing made of shiny satiny stuff. It had long, wide sleeves, and a picture of a dragon on the back. It was quite short. Katie's legs looked very long and tan; and her knees weren't knobbly anymore.

"What are you staring at, Dumbo?"

"Nothing," I said. It came out in a kind of croak. I cleared my throat. "Nothing," I repeated, in my normal voice. I perched on the edge of the bed. "So, what did Ivan Kingsley have to say?"

"Hang on, I can't hear you—wait till I've turned this thing off."

I sat and watched while she finished drying her hair. I couldn't remember ever seeing it loose before. It hung in a gleaming curtain, the color of gold. Her head was tilted slightly to the side; as she dried her hair, she stroked her brush through it, and it fell in a wonderful, heavy cascade, like a silken waterfall.

The edges of her Chinese dressing gown came together in a deep V at the front. As she turned to unplug the drier, I caught a flash of purest white lace, just the tiniest edge. I blushed and turned away.

"Push off while I get dressed; I won't be a sec."

I stumbled to my feet and blundered out, glad to get some air.

Two seconds later, Katie's door opened. She had on faded jeans and an outsize T-shirt that made her look very slim and fragile. It was black, and it had a little Scottie dog on the . . . where the front pocket would have been. The dog was making a fart shaped like a musical note.

"Cool T-shirt," I mumbled. Took my courage in my hands. "You look . . . pretty."

"Thanks," she said abruptly. I sat down on the arm of the sofa. I couldn't take my eyes off her.

"Uh . . . *Pi-ip* . . ." she began.

I took a quick breath and plunged in. "Hey, Katie—I was wondering if you'd . . . if we should go to the Igloo—to the Grand Opening? You and me?"

Katie looked away and bit her lip.

"And Michael," I added hurriedly.

Something's up, my brain said.

"I can't. I'm going out."

"Yeah? Where?" Maybe she was going to the mall—no problem, we could go straight on to the Igloo from there. Without Michael. I opened my mouth to suggest it, but Katie beat me to it.

"*Out* out."

"*Out* out?"

"As in, *out* with a . . . somebody. *That* kind of *out*."

The Earth dropped away from beneath my feet. I heard myself croak, "Who?"

"What d'you mean, *who*? What does it matter *who*? But, since you ask, Jordan Archer. And unless you want to bump into him on the doorstep . . ." She looked meaningfully at her watch.

Somehow I got myself back outside. On my way to the gate, I took one last look over my shoulder. Mrs. Wood was standing at the door, watching me. Even from that distance, I could see the look in her eyes. It was the exact same look Ivan Kingsley had given me.

JORDAN ARCHER

I stumbled home, straight to my room. Threw myself down on the bed. Started to pull my pillow over my head, out of habit. But then I stopped. Why bother? All the pillows in the universe wouldn't blot out the thought of Katie . . . and Jordan Archer.

Jordan was a year ahead of Nick at school—a senior. Like all the seniors, he wore long gray trousers instead of shorts, and a blazer and tie . . . and like most of the seniors, he pulled the tie down to half mast, and swaggered around with his hands in his blazer pockets and the sleeves pushed up to his elbows.

Jordan was taller than most of the teachers. He had broad shoulders and dark red hair Mum called auburn. She'd seen him once, when she was collecting me after school for a visit to the dentist. "Heavens, Pippin, who's that drop-dead gorgeous boy?" she'd asked. Mum, who never notices anything! "What a heartbreaker! And that auburn hair! Wasted on a boy . . . though perhaps not on that *particular* boy. Well, well—those seniors certainly are growing up!"

She didn't know Jordan Archer was a creep.

He hung out with these other guys who really prided themselves on their wit. They'd lounge around on the low wall near the side entrance, and keep up a running commentary on the other kids as they arrived for school. There'd be whistles for the pretty girls, and comments about their figures that made them blush. With plain girls—the chubby ones, or the ones with bad skin or glasses—they'd whisper to each other, then explode with laughter. Once, when Matilda Bunt walked past, Jordan Archer had barked like a dog. She just turned her head and walked faster; but when I got to class, she had her face deep in a book, and I could tell she was crying.

The girls weren't the only target of their "humor." They found pretty much everything funny—but the thing they found funniest was me and the milk run. It had started two terms ago, on a Monday morning—the day after Katie and Michael and I had been to the movies. Jordan had sat right behind us, crunching popcorn and making clever comments all the way through the movie. I guess he thought Katie and I were there together—*together* together, you know? At least, that was what I worked out later—because from that time on, he was constantly putting me down. When Katie wasn't around, that is.

The Monday after the movie, I was wheeling my bike through the gate, minding my own business. Suddenly I heard it: *"Moo!"* I was miles away and got such a fright I just about dropped my bike. I looked around and saw them: Jordan Archer and his friends. Lounging in a group—they were always in a group—up against the wall, hands in pockets, sniggering at me. Jordan's blazer collar was turned up.

"Would you look at that, fellas?" he said, in this mock-surprised voice. "It's *Moo McLeod*!"

His friends all fell over laughing.

I felt myself redden, and quickly looked away. That's what Mum always says: if someone teases you, ignore them. Then it won't be any fun for them, and they'll stop. But for Jordan and his friends, it was fun even when you ignored them. They were so endlessly entertained by their own cleverness, they didn't need a reaction to encourage them.

"*Moo!* Hey there, Moo McLeod! Moo Cow McLeod!"

"Hey, Moo Cow McLeod, why doncha get some balls?"

"Nah—*Moo Cow McLeod* thinks *balls* are a load of *bull*!"

Clever, huh? They thought so.

Problem was, girls seemed to think Jordan Archer was great. Some girls, anyhow. It was partly his looks, I guess. Plus, he had rich parents and lived in a big house at the top of the hill. And Jordan had his driver's license, and his own car. A beat-up old crock with a sawn-off exhaust; but hey—a car's a car.

To top it all, he was really good at sports. Nick said Jordan just narrowly missed getting onto the Highlands team for something—basketball, I think. I hadn't paid much attention at the time. Been short-listed; just missed out; and was a shoo-in for the team this year. Yeah, the final accessory

Jordan Archer needed to complete his image was a Highlands track top.

But it seemed as far as Katie was concerned, he didn't even need that.

Katie.

Katie, with her curtain of blond hair, her infectious grin, and her irreverent sense of humor. Katie, with her wicked left pass and her farting dog T-shirt.

Katie—*my* Katie.

The phone rang. Twice. Stopped.

Silence. Then Nick's bray: "Pipsqueak! Phone!"

Katie! She was calling to say it was all a joke—typical! She was calling to say she'd changed her mind—she wanted to come to the Igloo with me. With Michael and me, even. She was calling . . . she was calling . . . *she was calling!*

I was out of that room like a bullet; racing down the hall, skidding into the kitchen, thumping down on the sofa, taking a deep, steadying breath. Then: "Katie?"

"Pip—hi." Michael. "Hey, are we still going to the opening or what? I hadn't heard from you, so I thought I'd call and find out what you've arranged. Is Katie coming with us?"

Michael knew about Katie and me—sort of. I mean, I *think* he knew; and I think he knew I knew he knew. But Mike was cool, and he never said a word. And now, what was there to know?

"Hi Mike," I said dully. "No, Katie's . . . doing . . . something else."

"That's cool. I'll breeze by around five and pick you up. I've got my allowance; maybe there'll be somewhere we can buy an ice cream or something. Who knows? Hey—who knows *what* there'll be inside? See ya later!"

Bang—down went the phone.

In the end, I hadn't told anyone about my twilight visit. I would have, if it hadn't been for the climb, and that nightmare at the top of the Midnight Run. The whole thing seemed too intense and complex to share. Anyhow, I figured if old Ignatius Loon wanted it to be a surprise, then who was I to spoil his fun?

As Mike and I swooped through the open gate and cruised between the tightly packed rows of cars, I couldn't help feeling a twinge of excitement. It was all just how I'd imagined it—people everywhere; mums clutching toddlers' arms as they made desperate lunges in front of cars; the dome of the Igloo lit from inside with a pearly glow; neon signs splashing color into the gray evening; music spilling out of the huge double doors, open wide and crowded with people pushing and shoving and jostling and pointing.

I hugged the secret of my twilight visit close. In the deepest part of my mind, a single thought was cradled—as it had been for days—as private and perfect as a pearl in the heart of an oyster. *Climbing.*

We parked our bikes in the shiny new bike rack and clicked on their locks; then headed on in with the rest of the world.

The huge expanse of the ground floor was blazing with

light and buzzing with action. Demonstration matches were in full swing on all four indoor courts: cricket on one; soccer on two; basketball on the farthest. The grandstands were crowded with people. Now I could see the entrances— stretchy mesh openings that blended in so well with the walls that you only noticed them when people squeezed in and out. Officials were standing at each one, handing out pamphlets. Mike and I shoved our way over and took a couple; there were information brochures and enrollment forms and long, technical explanations of the rules of the different sports. I saw Nick over at the cricket game, deep in discussion with the organizer.

Then Mike was grabbing my arm and tugging me over to the Action Café, digging in his pocket for his wallet. That's Mike—he'd give you the shirt off his back. We ordered a burger each with all the trimmings, and some chips to share, and found a perch on the top of a grandstand to eat it.

Next we headed up to the second floor. Here, it seemed like every paunchy middle-aged man in town was lined up to enroll in the gym; we had a quick peek through the floor-to-ceiling glass windows, and every exercise machine known to man was in there, charged up and ready to go.

The entrance to the Action Bowling Alley was packed tight with people. Mike grabbed my arm, and we pushed and shoved and wriggled our way through the mob; until at last, standing on our toes and peering between the crush of bodies, we managed to catch a glimpse of polished wooden alleys, and hear the rattle and crash of falling pins. TVs above each lane showed awesome graphics of charging elephants and boxers being knocked out and racing cars spinning . . . and then the display would change to show how many pins had been knocked down and the configuration of the ones that were left. We watched with goofy grins plastered all over our faces.

Eventually I looked over at Mike, and he pointed up, eyebrows raised. I nodded: *Yes!* And up we went to the third floor.

It was definitely the coolest. Like the rest of the Igloo, the roof was made of hexagonal panels—but up here, the panels were transparent. The roof curved overhead like a gigantic glass bubble; through it, I could see darkness and just make out the misty sphere of the moon. In the daytime, sunlight would pour through—it would feel like being outdoors, only always warm, and protected from wind and rain. Awesome!

Almost the entire floor was taken up with two huge swimming pools. One was an Olympic-size pool, with lane dividers and podiums for the swimmers to dive from. The other was this wicked wave pool, with huge billows of water swooshing in gigantic tidal waves from the deep end. Kids on floatboards bobbed everywhere, shrieking with delight; fountains splashed; and at one side the pool narrowed into a river, with people floating and bobbing along, carried by the current.

I don't know how long Mike and I hung out up there, pointing and exclaiming and laughing and wishing we'd brought our swimming gear. At last, I looked at my watch.

Quarter to eight! I'd been due home at seven-thirty—Dad would kill me!

We made our way down to the ground floor, and my eyes slid to the entrance to the Climbing Center; I took a deep breath, still not sure what I was going to say. Mike grabbed my arm and pointed. "Hey, Pip—let's check that out! C'mon, another five minutes won't make much difference."

He dragged me across the room and through the wide open door into the passageway. This time, the door marked *Bouldering Room* was open. Inside was a magical mystery cave of climbing walls, some curving in and some curving out and some even upside down, all covered with hand- and footholds of every shape and size. The wall was about three times my height, and the floor was padded and squashy underfoot. Kids—big and little—clambered and squealed and tumbled everywhere. Mike was over at the wall in a flash, grinning over his shoulder; and I was right behind him.

After a couple of minutes, I checked my watch . . . and half an hour had gone by! I felt a lurch of horror—*Dad!*

"Mike!"

"Yeah, yeah, I know. Come on—one last look through here, and then we're off!"

I followed him down the passage toward the climbing stadium, my heart thumping with a strange mixture of excitement and dread. Deep down, I half-hoped it would be like it had been the other night—dark, mysterious, challenging. Logically, I knew it wouldn't be. But what if it were ordinary? What if the magic had gone?

Mike and I stepped through the entrance.

Bright light bathed the room, illuminating the walls and highlighting their brilliant colors and weird angles. Music blared from hidden speakers, drowning the babble of voices. The festoon of ropes was gone; instead, each individual climb had its own special safety rope secured far above, stretching down to a solid-looking anchor set into the floor.

Climbers were everywhere—clambering over the rock face like monkeys; dangling from ropes, spinning slowly as they were gradually lowered; rappelling down sheer drops; battling to cling onto impossible horizontal overhangs.

In the center of the large room was a raised, glass-covered block. A couple of intense guys in webbing harnesses were staring down at it, deep in discussion. Michael dragged me over, and I realized it was some kind of a map of the climbing routes. It hadn't been there three nights ago. My eyes scanned it, looking for the Midnight Run, trying to match the angular lines and weird names with the real-life walls rearing up all around me. Spaceboy . . . Tendon Teaser . . . Nutty Green Men . . . The Undertaker . . .

Suddenly, out of the corner of my eye, I saw something that made me forget about the Midnight Run. A slim figure perched on the edge of one of the benches, holding a can of soda. A slim figure in faded jeans and a black T-shirt, her eyes fixed on a point way above my head. Katie. I followed her gaze.

Jordan was a couple of meters from the top of the Midnight Run. *Jordan?* He was spread-eagled on the wall, his long, tanned legs tensed with effort and his neck craning upward as he looked for the next hold. He had on tight knee-length shorts and a vest that showed off his arm muscles, and was wearing a professional-looking harness with some kind of pouch attached to the back.

As I watched, he reached the top. Gave a signal to the guy below him, then let go and swung out from the wall, dangling from his rope like a spider from its web. Slowly, in a smooth, controlled drop, he was lowered toward the floor, his face alight with enjoyment . . . and his eyes fixed possessively on Katie, waiting for him below.

I swallowed, feeling sour bile rising up into my throat.

And then a voice spoke in my ear, almost making me jump out of my skin. "Hoped you'd be here tonight, Phil." I turned around, forcing my mouth into a smile. Rob Gale was grinning down at me. "Good to see you." He gestured with his chin. "That's Jordan Archer, one of our top junior climbers. He's been climbing over at the Y on the other side of town. Like the rest of us, he's over the moon about having this fantastic international-standard facility."

I croaked something—I wasn't sure what. It all came back to me now. *Climbing.* How could I have forgotten? Jordan Archer's sport was climbing. And now, here he was—with Katie looking like his biggest fan.

"I—I have to go," I stammered, desperate to leave before she saw me. Or—worse—before *he* did. Mike was over at the door, making faces and pointing at his watch.

"Hang on, Phil. Before you rush off—have you thought

about what I said the other night? About having a go at climbing? I was serious—even in those rather . . . *different* . . . circumstances." His eyes twinkled, and a smile tugged at the corner of his mouth. "We're running a beginners' class, every Wednesday at four for the next six weeks. How about it?"

"I—I can't." My face was burning; I was staring down at the map, praying for invisibility.

"Why not?"

"I can't afford it," I said lamely.

"Ah. That's okay, just come along to the first session and have a go—as my guest. No strings attached—only ropes!" He grinned. "Come on, Phil—what d'you say?"

I looked up at the Midnight Run. Deep down, I knew there was no choice. I ached to do it again—properly.

I had to.

"Wednesday?" I hedged. "Four o'clock?"

He nodded.

I slid a glance over at Jordan and Katie, tinkering with some kind of equipment with their backs to me.

If only Jordan . . .

"Jordan trains on Tuesdays and Thursdays," said Rob casually. Startled, I looked up at him. What made him say that? But he was gazing down at the map, deadpan. He couldn't have read anything on my face . . . could he?

"Okay," I heard myself say. "I'll be there."

He gave a satisfied nod. "Good. See you then."

"Rob . . ."

He turned back, one eyebrow raised.

"The Midnight Run—it isn't on the map."

His face lit up with that funny, lopsided grin. "Isn't it?"

I looked again. That was it, I was sure of it . . . but beside it, in red felt pen, the name *Phil's Folly.*

HOOKED

The truth was, somehow climbing seemed to have gotten into my blood. You'd expect that after what happened I'd have been put off for life. You'd expect the last thing I'd ever want to do would be to climb again.

But I thought about it all the time. I'd be sitting in math listening to Mr. Wells rabbiting on about algebra, or the Carling droning away about the food pyramid . . . and suddenly I'd be on the wall, my hands clamped to the holds, with an awesome feeling of adventure, challenge, and power coursing through me. I could replay whole sections of the climb in my mind. In my sleep I dreamed I was climbing, with a wonderful, tireless, gravity-defying ease; I'd wake exhausted, with my legs stiff and aching and my mind buzzing. I figured I was hooked. Maybe I had some kind of disease. Maybe I would cure it if I went back to the Igloo in the daytime, and had a boring old lesson with Rob, trussed up like a Christmas turkey with all those ropes and clips. That'd get it out of my system, for sure.

And in the meantime, it was a distraction from Katie, who seemed to be growing lovelier and more distant every day.

I counted the nights like a little kid, trying to speed up the clock by working extra hard on my homework, going to bed early, and getting in plenty of juggling practice. With just over a week to go to Mrs. Holland's D-day, I was a skilled hand with two mandarins, but hopeless with three. I either needed a major breakthrough, or some kind of miracle.

Finally it was Wednesday. I shot out the door mumbling that I might be late home from school; as I'd hoped, everyone was far too busy coping with the early morning madhouse to ask why.

That day seemed to last a century. But eventually the bell rang, and everyone headed for the bike sheds and freedom. Any other day, Mike would have been a problem—traditionally, we pushed our bikes up the hill together, moaning about teachers, grouching about homework, and generally planning for the weekend. But he was staying late for a meeting about the new photography club, so it was easy for me to slip away alone, and turn off toward the Igloo instead of up the hill and home.

I parked my bike alongside a couple of others in the rack, a sick feeling tweaking my gut. *What if it isn't how I remember it? What if Rob says I'm no good? What if the magic doesn't happen again?*

I padded through the big double doors. Games were underway on the indoor courts; there were people around, but nothing like the day of the opening. I barely spared them a glance. Checked my watch: five to four. Went on through, down the corridor, past the Bouldering Room, into the main climbing gym.

It was practically empty: ropes set for climbing stretched floor to ceiling, and one of the local radio stations played softly from the invisible speakers.

A couple of kids about my age were hanging around looking lost. Over on one side I could see Rob, his blond ponytail tangled against a faded track top, sorting out gear from one of the metal lockers.

A stocky, dark-haired boy gave me an uncertain, slightly nervous grin. "You here for the course?"

I nodded.

"Beginners' top rope," said one of the girls, with a superior smile. "I've done it before, two years ago at the Y— this is just a refresher for me, before I graduate to leading."

Leading? My heart sank. Was this going to be another competition thing, with leaders and followers, winners and losers? I realized part of the magic for me had been that, like juggling, climbing seemed like something you could just *do*—for the sheer love of it.

"Okay, guys, gather 'round," Rob called.

Obediently, we trailed across to where he was standing.

"Help yourselves to climbing shoes from the rack—the

sizes are pretty much standard. Grab a harness, too—we'll run through how to put them on, and the basics of safety and belaying."

The girl put her hand up. "I already know all that. Can't I—"

"I'm afraid not," Rob interrupted. "This is a group lesson, and that means you move at the pace of the group. You're Sharon, aren't you—the girl who wanted the refresher? Well, stick around, pin your ears back, and get refreshed. Safety is one issue you can't go over often enough."

Slowly, step by step, he demonstrated how to put the harnesses on—uncomfortable straps that fitted around your waist and thighs, tightening with buckles till they were firm and snug.

Next, we moved over to the climbing wall, and Rob showed us how to tie the harness onto the rope. "Most of the time, the rope is hardly used," he explained. "But it's vital to remember that if you get the knot wrong and something unexpected happens, someone could die." We all exchanged solemn glances. "Climbing is essentially an individual sport," Rob went on, "but it's also unique in the extent to which you rely on your climbing companions. This is particularly true of top roping, where the climber relies on the belayer to limit the distance of a fall, should one happen. Now, anyone know what belaying is?"

Sharon's hand shot up.

"Sharon?"

"It's where you like . . . have to stand at the bottom of the wall and . . . uh . . ." Rob waited. "It's kind of . . . hard to describe," she finished lamely.

"Thank you, Sharon." I thought I saw a glint of laughter in Rob's eyes, but his face was serious as he continued. "Belaying is the process of holding and managing the rope from below in such a way that you safeguard your fellow climber. Just like when you tie knots, at times you literally have your partner's life in your hands. Belaying is both a science and an art, and good belayers are worth their weight in gold. Today we're going to learn the basics . . . and climb a few walls and have a lot of fun! Okay—each of you grab a partner!"

The stocky boy and I exchanged a glance and shuffled closer together. The others paired off, too. "I'm Darren," he said.

"Phil," I told him, with a quick grin. It was getting easier. Who knows—one day maybe I'd even feel like it was true.

"Hope you're a good belayer," he whispered.

"Same here," I told him, and we both grinned.

Then Rob was off again, keeping it simple, taking it step by step. And before I knew it, I was braced and anchored at the foot of the wall, eyes fixed on Darren as he put his hands and feet on the first holds and hoisted himself upward to start his first climb.

We were all on easy climbs first time around—Darren's and mine, Climb Number 5, was reassuringly called Stroll in the Park, I noticed with a private smile. I was starting to detect Rob's sense of humor in the names, though I hardly knew him.

Watching Darren as he worked his way cautiously up the wall, I itched for my turn. From where I stood, craning upward, my neck starting to ache and the rope playing smoothly through my hands, I could see exactly where the next handhold was, where I'd put my foot if it were me. Suddenly I understood just how Kwong must feel. He's this math genius in our class who knows all the answers before Mr. Wells has even finished writing out the question. While the rest of us sit there scratching our heads, staring at the ceiling and longing for the bell, Kwong wriggles around in his chair as if it's red hot, trying desperately to stop himself from yelling out the answer.

For me, watching Darren clamber slowly up that wall, it felt just the same. *Steady on*, I told myself. *It's easy from the bottom, when you're not the one climbing. Wait till it's you up there, smart aleck!*

At long last, Darren reached the top and looked down, his face one gigantic grin of triumph. I checked that the rope was in the right position to lower him safely, then called to him; and he swung out from the rock face with a whoop, spinning 'round and 'round as I lowered him gently to the floor.

And then it was my turn.

We switched places. Finally, roped up and ready to go, I was standing at the foot of the wall. I dusted some chalk onto my hands from the pouch at my waist, took a deep breath, and began to climb.

An hour and a half later—an eternity or a second later, it would have been all the same to me—we were undoing our harnesses and untying our shoes. The shy, awkward silence at the start of the session had dissolved into an excited babble:

"Hey, did you see me on that overhang? I reckon next time I'll make it for sure!"

"I'd have cracked it, no problem, if my hand hadn't slipped on that last hold!"

"Did you try number twelve—Lover's Leap? It's impossible, man—no one could climb that unless they had suckers on their feet!"

The voices swirled and eddied around me like water.

I didn't say anything. Couldn't. I was still battling to come down to Earth. For the first time, I understood the saying: *Down to Earth*. Down from the clouds . . . down from the moon . . . down to where gravity took hold, and real life kicked in.

"Phil?"

Automatically, feeling dazed and moving like a sleep-walker, I stashed my climbing shoes and harness and headed for the door.

"Phil!"

Oh yeah—that's me. Reluctantly, I turned back. Rob was standing at the locker, a tangle of harnesses in one hand. "Hang fire a sec, I'd like a word."

I went over, my feet feeling stiff and clumpy, as if I were wearing lead boots. My heart felt like lead, too. I didn't want to talk to Rob. I needed some time on my own, to figure out some way to scrape together the non-existent funds to finance climbing once a week. I'd seen the other kids pay over crumpled ten-dollar bills. For our family, ten dollars might as well be ten thousand. It was just as impossible.

"Do you need some help?" I heard myself ask. My voice sounded strange and hollow, as if it belonged to someone else.

"Nope—just about done."

I watched the last figures straggle off through the door, snatches of their exuberant, excited voices wafting back as they disappeared.

Rob closed the locker door and leaned back against it, arms folded. His wide mouth had an odd quirk; his eyes were smiling and very blue. He looked at me for what seemed a long time, without saying a word.

I shuffled my feet, looked down, then back up at him. At last, in spite of myself, I smiled back. "What?" I asked grudgingly.

"I think you know what," he replied. "Sit here next to me for a sec. We need to talk."

I perched next to him on one of the long steel benches. He swiveled to face me, becoming serious. "Phil," he said, "I've been climbing for close on fifteen years. Started when I was ten. And I've been coaching pretty much since I left school."

There was an intensity about his eyes that made me focus on every word. I sensed that what he was about to say was important . . . maybe the most important thing I'd ever hear in my life.

"More than a few climbers have passed through my hands in that time. Ordinary kids, like today . . . rich kids with money to burn on swanky equipment and parents desperate to keep them off the streets . . . kids with climbing in their blood . . . even some with real talent. Kids like Jordan Archer, who have the potential to go a fair way with a lot of hard work, the right attitude, and a little luck."

He paused again, looking for words. "I've never seen a climber to touch you, Phil. It's that simple. I look at you, and I see myself when I was a kid—but better than I ever was. You know it, don't you?"

I swallowed. My heart was beating in my throat; I didn't know if the words would come out. But I tried. "I know . . . I know this is what I want to do. Not eat, or sleep, or play soccer, or go to school, or anything. Just this. Just climb." He nodded, encouraging me to go on. "But how can you tell? I mean—what you said? About me being . . . I mean, I've only climbed this once. How *can* you know?"

He smiled: a smile full of a certainty I suddenly knew I could trust absolutely. "I know. Good climbers—great climbers—have the flow. When they climb, everything comes together, and their body just ripples up the rock. It's fluidity; it's rhythm; it's like dancing up the wall. It never happens for most climbers. Others train for years before they achieve it." He looked me straight in the eyes. "I saw a glimmer of it the other night, when you were climbing down the Midnight Run. And I saw it again today.

"You were born to climb. What we need to discuss now is not whether, or why. It's simply how, and when."

THE THIRD MANDARIN

Sunday lunch. Mum's homemade hamburgers, with sliced tomato, pickles, fried onions, whole-grain mustard, and lashings of tomato sauce.

Nick was on his third. I was still on my first, keeping a watchful eye on the last meat patty. It had my name on it, I reckoned; but I knew that if he had half a chance, my brother would whip it from under my nose.

"So anyway," Nick was saying, taking a slice of cheese and adding it to his creation, which already looked like the Leaning Tower of Pisa, "this guy Brent, who organizes the indoor cricket, said he'd get back to me once they'd finished going through the applications. But there'd definitely be vacancies for umpires, especially on Friday nights. That's their big night; they have this league . . ."

I nibbled at the frilly edge of lettuce sticking out from my bun, and licked away the dollop of mustard squishing out below. *I've never seen a climber to touch you.* It was as if

Rob's words were engraved on my heart. When I died, I wanted them carved on my tombstone.

Could it be true? Could I have something . . . special? Something Rob had never seen before? It seemed like some kind of fantastic dream . . . because this was me we were talking about. Pip McLeod—no, *Phil* McLeod.

It was unbelievable. And yet, at the same time, I knew it was true. I could feel it, with a kind of recognition—a weird, primitive, instinctive knowledge that had more to do with my heart than my brain.

"You don't belong in this class, for starters," Rob had told me. "I'd like to move you to the transition class I'm running on Fridays. It's a small group of kids about your own age, some a bit older. Varying abilities—they've just completed an advanced top-rope class, and are ready to move on. You'll catch up any slack, no problem—the emphasis in this class is on individual development, so it'll be perfect for you."

"But Rob . . . what about . . ." I'd swallowed, scared to say the word, terrified the bubble would burst. But I had no choice. "The problem is money. We don't have any." It was out. The end of everything . . . before it had even begun.

Rob just smiled. "You know who the Igloo's named after, don't you? Ignatius Loon, the eccentric millionaire recluse who lived in a tumbledown bungalow in the old housing estate?" I nodded. "The neighborhood kids called him Old Loony, apparently. You can imagine them, can't you?

Jogging down the footpath after him as he struggled along in his wheelchair, chanting their taunts." I could imagine it all too well. "Most people would've wanted to wring their necks—me, for one. But not Ignatius Loon. Instead, he left them a sporting facility that rivals the best in the country. And he left something else, too . . . something that hasn't been publicized.

"Ignatius Loon set up a series of grants to enable local kids to receive special coaching they wouldn't otherwise be able to afford. Kids like the ones who used to jeer at him; kids with no money, or not much; kids with talent, *real* talent. The Ignatius Loon Discretionary Sporting Scholarships—bit of a mouthful, huh? They've been established in all the sporting areas the Igloo covers—soccer, cricket, basketball, swimming, bowling . . . and climbing. No big fanfare; no big deal. Just the funding to enable special kids to follow their dreams . . . courtesy of a man who was never able to pursue his own. Kids like you."

So it had all been decided. "I'll give your folks a call," Rob said, "and let them know the score."

"*No!*" I heard myself saying. "No! You . . . I . . . *Dad* . . ." Panic flared through me like flame blazing through dry brush. I fought it down. "I'd rather tell them myself," I managed at last. "It'll be . . . like . . . a real cool surprise, you know? They'll be fine about it all—they'll be really, *really* pleased."

And that was how we'd left it. Rob didn't know I had no intention of telling them, or anyone else. Not about the climbing; not about the scholarship; not about any of it.

This was one thing I wasn't going to let Dad anywhere near. This was mine. It had nothing to do with comparing and competing, with winning and losing. It had nothing to do with trying to be best, and that sick feeling of failure when my best was never enough. This was about me. I wasn't doing it for Mum, or Dad, or a Highlands track top, or even for Rob.

I was doing it for myself.

I'd lost sleep worrying about how to explain away my absences on Friday afternoons. I realized that, no matter how I swung it, it would involve . . . not lying, exactly, more a kind of gentle bending of the truth. I felt bad about it, for Mum especially. But she was the one who was always saying *you can't make an omelet without breaking eggs*. These eggs wouldn't even really be broken—just slightly cracked. I'd decided on my strategy; and choosing the exact right moment was the most important part.

"So yesterday evening, the phone rings," Nick was saying. "And I go, 'Hello?' And this voice at the other end goes, 'Good afternoon, is that Nicholas McLeod?' And I'm wondering, who the heck can *this* be? And then the guy goes: 'This is Brent, from the Igloo, phoning about your application for a part-time job as an indoor cricket umpire!'" Nick paused for effect, taking a massive bite of burger and keeping us all in suspense while he chewed it.

Burger! I checked the platter. It was empty. "Hey,

that was *mine*! I've only had one!"

Nick swallowed. "And I'm like, *Jeez, will ya get to the point!* Only I don't say that, of course. I play it real cool. And then he goes, 'We've reviewed all the applications,'—that's how he talks, real stuffy—'and we're delighted to offer you the position, Fridays from five-thirty to eight!' And I'm: *Yeah! Way to go! Far out, man!* But all I say is, 'Thank you, Brent,' real laidback and polite. And then he goes, 'I dare say you'll be wondering about money.'"

Another bite of burger. *My* burger. Well, I reckoned there'd never be a better moment.

I cleared my throat and said, kind of softly, as if I'd been thinking about something entirely different from what Nick was going on about: "I was thinking I might join the photography club."

"Well?" growled Dad. "How much is it? More than the paper route?"

"Fifteen dollars an hour!" crowed Nick triumphantly. "So that's . . . if you work it out . . ."

"That's wonderful, sweetheart," Mum said to Nick. Then, to me: "When is it?"

Nick: "I just told you! Fridays, five-thirty till eight! So that's two and a half hours, at fifteen dollars an hour: thirty-seven dollars and fifty cents! Way more than I make on my paper route—in just one evening! And there's the chance of more time slots further down the track; and maybe even soccer reffing, too!"

"Fridays," I mumbled. "Fridays, right after school."

"Would you be back for the milk run?" growls Dad.

"What milk run?" asked Nick, looking confused. "My paper route, d'ya mean? *Da-ad*, that's the whole point! I'd give *up* the paper route! I'd have to, but it wouldn't matter, 'cause I'd make way more money. . . ."

"Yeah, Dad," I said gloomily. "I'd be back in time for the milk run."

Mum fetched the fruit bowl and put it down in the middle of the table. "I'll tell you one thing," she said: "I'm not buying fruit from that greengrocer on the corner again. Those mandarins looked lovely, but the whole lot have turned to mush. They must have been bruised."

"Yeah—I took one yesterday, and my finger went straight through it. And when I turned it over, it was stuck to the bowl with this furry gray fuzz. Yee-uck!" said Nick.

I felt myself flush. "Maybe it wasn't the greengrocer's fault," I muttered guiltily. Mum gave me a look.

Dad shoved his chair back from the table. "Well, I'm off to the depot to stock up on the new line. Banana custard. A real money-maker—so they say."

Nick honked with laughter. "Banana custard? Hey, Pipsqueak—what's yellow and dangerous?"

"I dunno."

"Shark-infested custard! And hey, how about this one? What's yellow and gives you nits in your armpits?" Nick, high on the excitement of his new job, was capering around the table, scratching under his arms and jibbering like a circus chimp. But he'd failed to notice the warning signs—

Dad's mustache was starting to bristle, his bushy brows were drawing together, and his wrinkle barometer was signaling clearly *storm ahead—run for cover.* "MooZical Milk's new *Banana custard!* Bananas—monkeys—get it?" Nick hooted, without even waiting for an answer. "Hey, Dad—you'll need a marketing gimmick. *Free pack of nits with every carton*, how about that? They'd—"

Dad stood up, his chair clattering over onto the floor. "Right. Since you take such an interest in the business, Nicholas, you can come with me for the afternoon. To the depot, top-to-toe spring clean of the milk truck, inside and out. No arguments. Pip—you can stay home and look after your sister while your mother does the shopping. And make sure you're here at five—I want to start the run on time."

"Hey, Dad," I said unwisely, "I was wondering: if Nick's giving up his paper route, couldn't I—"

"No!" yelled Dad, and slammed out, leaving the kitchen as hollow and silent as the calm in the eye of a tornado.

"Don't you boys *ever* learn?" asked Mum, starting to clear the table. Nick, looking sheepish, followed reluctantly in Dad's turbulent wake. I started to help Mum, looking as hangdog as possible. But inside, my heart was singing.

The moment had passed . . . and I doubted anyone had even noticed. I had my Friday afternoons. *I'd done it!*

"Now I want you to concentrate. Concentration is the key. That's how I learned to juggle two oranges: by concentrating."

I fetched a pack of raisins from the pantry, and held them up for her to see. Moved them left . . . right . . . up . . . down. Madeline's eyes followed them faithfully: left . . . right . . . up . . . down.

"Good! Good girl!" I lifted her down from her highchair, and sat her gently on the floor. "Now, Madeline, look!" With exaggerated movements, like a magician producing a rabbit from a hat, I picked out one raisin and held it up just above her. "See the yummy raisin?" I waved it back and forth; then slowly, making sure she was watching, I put it down . . . on the very edge of the sofa. *"Raisin!"* I said.

Madeline had just finished lunch, but she loved raisins. She hitched herself closer to the sofa on her butt, craning her neck to try and see where the raisin had gone. "It's on the sofa," I told her. *"Up* on the sofa."

She'd reached the front of the sofa now and was holding out her arms, fat little hands stretched wide like pink starfish. "Uppy tofa!" she said, looking first at me, then at the sofa. "Daisin. *Pease* daisin?"

"No," I explained. "If you want it, you'll have to get it yourself. I know it sounds mean, but in the long run, you'll thank me for it." That was something Dad always said: *In the long run, you'll thank me for it.* I didn't like hearing his words coming out of my mouth. I wished I could suck them back. Next thing I knew, I'd be saying: You have to be the *best* walker, Madeline—*the very best!*

But Madeline hadn't noticed; or if she had, she didn't care. She was too busy pulling herself up to get the raisin.

Up, so she was standing, her fat little tummy squashed against the front of the sofa, one hand clutching on tightly, the other reaching for the raisin. She'd done it! Madeline had stood up, all by herself!

If Madeline could do it, so could I. After all, she had the rest of her life to learn to walk, but I had less than a week to learn to juggle three oranges.

No one had touched the mandarins at lunch—I think they'd been put off by Nick's description of the gray fuzz. There were four left. I chose the firmest three. I held two in one hand, one in the other. I threw the first mandarin from the "two" hand up in a gentle arc. Then, when it reached the top of its arc, I threw the single mandarin up, so they crossed over. When it reached the top of its arc, I threw up mandarin number three—and the whole lot fell on the floor.

Madeline laughed and rocked forward onto her hands and knees, trundling after them as they rolled away across the kitchen. I grabbed them quickly, before she could get hold. Madeline could do terrible things to an orange, especially a squishy one.

I tried again. This time, I didn't rush my second throw. I tried to get a feel—the same rhythmic feel that had suddenly happened with two oranges in the steamy bathroom the other night. I tried again . . . and again . . . and again. And suddenly it happened!

I got such a fright, I lost it; the mandarins tumbled to the floor again, rolling away under the table. Madeline was after them like a bloodhound.

"No, Madeline, no!" I told her. "I need them. I've cracked it—did you see? Were you watching? Look, you can have a grandstand seat." I lifted her up and sat her on the sofa with her raisins. "Now, watch this." I only half-believed it would work; only half-believed I could do it. But I held them. Focused. Concentrated.

One . . . two . . . *three*.

The mandarins flowed from hand to hand, tracing smooth arcs through the air in a perfect cascade . . . again, and again, and again.

This time, when I lost the rhythm and they thudded to the floor, I lifted Madeline down and let her chase after them. We'd both done enough for one day. We'd each achieved a major breakthrough.

We played the Mandarin Game together, throwing those oranges around the kitchen floor, crawling after them, grabbing them, rolling them and tossing them, until my knees were sore and my sides hurt from laughing, and Madeline was way past her use-by date and ready for her nap.

ALGEBRA WITH KATIE

After dinner, my door blew open and Nick breezed in—without knocking, same as always. I'd been lying on the bed with a book open beside me, daydreaming. Dreaming of climbing . . . dreaming of Katie. Dreaming of juggling not two, not three or even four, but five mandarins.

When Nick came in, I quickly picked up my book and pretended I'd been reading. But you can never fool Nick.

"So—moping, Pipsqueak?" He crossed over to my desk and picked up my mechanical pencil. I watched him warily out of the corner of my eye. Typical Nick—won't let me into his room without a straightjacket; then barges into mine, and immediately starts fiddling with all my stuff.

"No," I said defensively. "Why would I be moping?" He gave me a sly sideways grin, pressed the clicker at the end of the pencil, and pulled the thin lead out so it looked like an injection needle. "Nick—those leads break real easy. And that's my last one."

"I reckon anyone'd mope in your shoes, Pipsqueak. What

with Jordan stealing your girlfriend and parading her all over town."

I felt like he'd punched me in the stomach. "Katie's not my girlfriend!"

"Well, then, I guess you won't care who she goes out with, huh?" He slid the lead back into the pencil. There was the tiniest *snick* as it snapped. Nick tossed the broken part—the longest part—toward the wastepaper basket, and missed.

Questions were banging around in my head like pool balls: *Who told you? Is she "going out" with Jordan officially? Where has he been "parading" her?* And the biggest question: *Was she my girlfriend? Had she ever been? Was that the way things worked—that someone could be your girlfriend without you even realizing it? Or was it just Nick, stirring things up?*

"Guh," I said.

"Yeah, guh," agreed Nick. "That's pretty much how I'd feel about it, too, if I was you. Still, you'll have her back eventually. Girls don't last long with Jordan. He has this real short attention span where they're concerned—he's not too interested in getting to know them, or any of that kind of stuff." He picked up my key ring—the rubber hippo with the big brown turd that bulges out its butt when you press its sides. The key ring Katie gave me last birthday.

"Put that down!" I snapped.

Nick put it down, giving me an injured look. "Yeah," he said thoughtfully, rifling through the stuff on my desk on his search-and-destroy mission, "when it comes to girls, Jordan's only after one thing. Once he's got it, he'll throw the leftovers back, no worries."

A hot, bitter taste like vomit rose up into my throat. I fought it down. *One thing?* "What thing?" I croaked, not wanting to know the answer.

Nick slouched to the door, tossing my rocket-bounce ball from hand to hand. "Take it from me: you don't want to know, baby bro. Just take comfort from the fact that it won't last long. Jordan doesn't really care about her—that guy doesn't care about anyone except himself. She's just another scalp to add to his collection."

On the way out, he paused, as if he'd had a sudden thought. Then: "Tell you what, though, Pipsqueak. If it was me, I wouldn't let her go without a fight. She's pretty cool, that Katie. Too cool for Jordan." He gave me a wink and tossed the bouncy ball at me. Cruised out again, leaving the door wide open—and the contents of my desk and my thoughts in turmoil.

Then, biking to school, Michael started in on me. It turned out he'd known all along. "So what's with Katie?" he asked out of the blue, freewheeling beside me with his eyes fixed on the road ahead.

"Katie?" I hedged.

"Yeah, Katie. Ever heard of her?"

"I—uh—how d'you mean?"

Mike took his eyes off the road long enough to give me a look. A world-weary look I'd seen on his face many times before—a look he once admitted he'd spent hours perfecting in front of the mirror. It was an integral part of his image . . .

but it was the first time he'd ever directed it at me. "Play it that way if you want, Romeo. But I reckon you had something going there for a while. And now, maybe you blew it."

I was stung. "*I blew it?* What d'you mean? It's not my fault if Katie decides to go out with someone. I don't own her. We're just friends."

"Oh, right, just friends, huh? *Sor-ry*, but somehow that bit escaped my notice." Sarcasm is another of Mike's weapons that hadn't been aimed at me before. I flinched, not enjoying being the target. I had an awful premonition that we were on the verge of a fight. I'd already lost one best friend—what if I lost the other?

And then it all clicked into place: Mike was doing it because he didn't know how else to deal with the situation. He was as uncomfortable with all this girl stuff as I was—he was worried about me and trying to help.

I gulped, feeling a great lump of pride making its slow, reluctant way down my gullet like cold mashed potatoes. "I don't know what to do," I confessed. "About Katie. For a while, I thought we were . . . you know?" Mike swerved around a stone, frowning. I could tell he was listening. "And then, suddenly, out of nowhere, this thing with Jordan." I hadn't said much; but I knew that for Michael, it would be enough. "So now, I don't know what to do," I repeated numbly.

"Have you talked to her?"

"Huh?"

"Have you talked to her? Have you, like, discussed it?"

"Discussed what?"

"Told her . . . like . . . how you feel? About her—and

about this whole Jordan drama. Maybe she doesn't even know. Maybe you *thought* she knew, but all the time, she didn't. Maybe she just got tired of waiting."

My brain spun. Not know? How could Katie not have known? But then . . . I'd taken so much trouble to hide how I felt. Yeah! Of course she didn't know! *And if she did?* If she suddenly *did* know—*if I told her*—what then?

"But I can't tell her," I muttered. "What would I say? I haven't spoken to her for days."

A horrible image swum into my mind of me kneeling at Katie's feet holding up a red rose. I squeezed my eyes shut to get rid of it. *"Look out!"* squawked Mike. I opened my eyes just in time to dodge the lamppost bearing down on me.

"You'll find a way," said Mike, as we slowed down for the traffic light. "I think you should give it a go, you poor, pathetic excuse for a human being. Then, even if she tells you to get lost, at least you'll know you tried."

So. Seemed like everyone thought I should talk to Katie. Everyone . . . even me. Talk to Katie! Such a short time ago, it had been something I'd done every day, without even noticing. Now it loomed ahead like a solo attempt on Mount Everest.

Without oxygen.

During our math test, I decided the sooner, the better. So much of it had been just in my mind—what if the new distance that had sprung up between us was in my mind, too? Katie was probably wondering what the problem was. Maybe she hadn't even noticed there was a problem. Maybe she and Jordan were just friends. Yeah, there was no doubt about it. We needed to talk.

My guts writhed painfully at the thought. *Are you sure this is wise?* asked my brain. *Sharrup!* I growled. *Mind your own damn business!*

I phoned Katie on Tuesday afternoon at eight minutes past four. Tuesday, because I needed the whole of Monday to think out my strategy; and anyhow, Monday seemed a bit soon. After four, to give her time to get home from school and have her afternoon snack, but not get too engrossed in her homework. The old Katie had never minded having her homework interrupted; but maybe the new one was different. And eight minutes past . . . well, because it had the casual, spontaneous feel of someone who just happened to be passing the phone and thought *Hey! I'll give old Katie a call!*

I dialed . . . but then, just before I got to the final number, I quickly hung up. I checked that no one was around and closed my bedroom door. The last thing I needed was Nick to come in while I was on the phone, even though I wasn't planning on talking for long.

All clear. I swallowed, took a deep breath, and dialed again. The phone rang once . . . twice. If I listened hard enough, I could hear it ringing distantly next door.

"Hello?" her voice sounded slightly breathless; excited.

"Katie?" I croaked.

"Oh. It's you."

"Hi!"

"Hi."

"So . . . uh . . . what've you been up to?" I asked.

"What do you mean?"

"Oh, you know . . . I just wondered . . . well, I just wondered . . . how you are."

"How I am? I'm fine."

"Uh—don't you want to know how I am?"

"I already know how you are. I saw you at school about an hour and fifteen minutes ago. Unless there's a bout of bubonic plague sweeping through Hillcrest, I assume you're about the same now as you were then. Which seemed fine."

"Yeah, right, I *am* fine, actually." Somehow this conversation wasn't going the way I'd planned. I needed to take control! "Katie . . ."

"What?"

"I wondered . . . if you aren't too busy . . . whether you'd like to go down to the park; maybe pick up an ice cream?" I'd already raided my battered old money-box. I checked that the coins were still there in my pocket. They chinked encouragingly.

A sigh gusted down the line. "I'm on a diet."

Katie on a *diet*?

"Oh, yeah, right . . . a diet. Sure. Well . . ." sudden inspiration . . . "how about a diet soda?"

A snort of laughter came down the line—a glimpse of the

old Katie, the one who'd guzzle double-thick milkshakes and chocolate bars for breakfast, lunch, and dinner if she had the chance.

"Come on, just a quick one?" I added, pressing home my advantage.

"All right—but it'll have to be quick. I haven't started my homework."

Half an hour later, we were sitting on the metal dividers of the rusty old merry-go-round at the park, going around in slow circles. In more ways than one.

We'd stopped off at the corner store on the way. I'd chosen a Tex Bar, even though I didn't really like them. I thought the macho, gun-slinging sound of it fitted the situation, the image of myself I wanted to convey. Phil McLeod, a man's man, a force to be reckoned with. Not the kind of guy to buy a Pixie Bar, or a box of Tweeties.

Katie had chosen a Peppermint Crisp chocolate ice, and checked whether I could afford it. Both good signs, I reckoned.

Before, we would have exchanged bites. Now, we each nibbled our own in pensive silence. At last, emboldened by my Tex Bar, I took the bull by the horns. "So," I said, very casual, "how's it going with Jordan?"

Instantly, Katie's face took on a closed, wary look. "Jordan? Have you asked me here so you can talk about Jordan?"

"No, of course not—why would I?" I backtracked hurriedly. "I just happened to ask . . . to make conversation, you know . . ."

"Well, don't," she said.

'Round and 'round we went. 'Round and 'round went my thoughts. I was starting to feel slightly sick. Katie's tongue licked the last smooth swathe of ice cream off the stick. Her tongue was pink and pointed at the end, like a cat's. She closed her eyes like a cat when she licked, too.

She opened them again and gave me a brisk, business-like smile. "Well," she said, "thanks for the ice cream. And now I'd better go and do my homework."

"Hang on—wait!" I'd just about got down to the biscuit layer under the chocolate. The sick feeling was worse. "Katie . . . we . . . need to talk."

She frowned. "No, we don't."

"Yeah, we do. Just listen for a second. What I want to say—well, it's important."

She rolled her eyes, sighed, and leaned back against the metal bar. She folded her arms and looked at me. "Okay," she said. "Talk."

My entire life flashed past my eyes like a sped-up movie, like they say happens when you're drowning. I closed my eyes for a second, took a deep breath, opened them again, and plunged in. Sink or swim.

"Katie . . . you know you and Jordan, right?" The frown again. I held up my hands, like I was surrendering. "Hang on, hear me out. I'm not asking—I mean, it's none of my business. But think of it in terms of, say . . . algebra. Where symbols represent different things, right? Well, say your . . . relationship . . . with Jordan, say that was, like, a B-type relationship. And your friendship—I mean your *relationship*—

with me: well, up till now it's been like a kind of an A-type relationship. Would you agree with that?"

Katie was staring at me with a kind of dazed look. I had an instant of wild hope—yeah! She hadn't known! It was all going to be okay!

"So anyhow," I soldiered on, "what I wondered is: why don't we try out a B-type relationship? You and me?"

"Are you saying what I think you're saying?"

"No! Well . . . yes, probably. Maybe. I'm not talking about a fully fledged B-type relationship; just an A-type relationship with a slight B spin on it. Just at first, till we see what develops."

Katie shook her head slowly from side to side, as if she wasn't believing what she was hearing.

She isn't going for it, warned my brain.

Hang on, I told it. *Let's just see. She needs a bit of time to get used to the idea.*

She didn't.

"Pip," she said. I used to hate Katie calling me Piphead, but I'd have given anything to hear her say it now. "You're overlooking one thing. The feelings I have for Jordan are B-type feelings. Feelings I could never in a million years have for you."

"But—how do you know . . . unless you've tried?"

"Believe me, I know."

I felt things slipping away—the conversation, the whole situation, and any faint remaining hope I might have had.

"But Katie—"

"Put yourself in my position. Could *you* have B-type feelings for Matilda Bunt?"

Matilda Bunt! Did Katie see me as a male version of Matilda Bunt? I felt the blood rush to my face. "Well, now that you put it like that . . . I guess not," I admitted stiffly.

"There you are then!" said Katie triumphantly. "Relationships aren't algebra—and even if they were, some combinations don't add up. As far as you and me are concerned, it's an A-type relationship or nothing. Take your pick."

Unlike Ivan Kingsley or Mrs. Wood, there wasn't a shred of pity in Katie's eyes.

She turned on her heel and walked away, the ice-cream stick clenched in her fist.

I sat there on the merry-go-round watching her go, shriveled up inside like one of Madeline's raisins.

LICORICE

"This is Trixie," said Rob. "Trixie, Phil. Trixie's without a partner, so the two of you can work together for today. Trix has had a fair bit of experience on top roping, and a couple of weeks on leading. You'll muddle along fine, I'm sure. Get yourselves roped up and we'll be underway."

My heart sank. This was worse than the Carling and her cooking class—the last thing I wanted was to be paired off with a girl! And looking at Trixie's face, I could see she felt exactly the same about me.

Trixie? What kind of a name was that? It conjured up visions of a delicate doll-like creature with flossy gossamer hair and a heart-shaped face—a kind of human poodle.

But this Trixie reminded me of a troll. She was small and chunky-looking, with a square, bad-tempered face under a helmet of dark hair. Her black eyes glared at me from under her heavy bangs as if I were Public Enemy Number One.

I gave her a wary smile, which she didn't return. Hurriedly, I looked away, and started doing up my harness.

The buckles were stiff, and my fingers felt clumsy and awkward. I could feel her watching my every move, hostility and contempt radiating from her in almost visible waves.

Eventually I was finished, and we moved off to the climb Rob had allocated to us: number 16, The Turtle Wins the Race. "It has that name for a very good reason." Rob grinned cheerfully down at our glum faces. "Any idea what it is?" Trixie set her mouth in a stubborn line and didn't answer.

Knowing it wouldn't do anything to increase my popularity, I answered, "Is it like the Hare and the Tortoise? You have to, like, take it slowly?"

Rob gave me a grin and thumbs-up. "Right on, Phil. Slow and easy. It isn't a hard climb, but there are a couple of tricky bits, as you'll discover. I want you both to climb it once on the top rope; I'll keep an eye on you and see how you cope. Then perhaps we'll start you off on leading toward the end of the session, Phil—but on an easier climb. Away you go."

I'd done my homework in the school library, and now I knew what Rob was talking about. In lead climbing, instead of relying on a top rope up above to hold you if you fell, you fastened special clips called carabiners onto metal bolts pre-set into the wall as you climbed. The rope went through them and back down to the belayer below. It had nothing to do with winning and losing—if anything, it gave you more independence and responsibility in your climbing. I couldn't wait to try it . . . but I would have given anything for a different partner.

"Well," muttered Trixie at the bottom of the climb, "want to go first?"

"Thanks," I said, surprised.

"Don't worry," she sneered, "I won't let you fall."

"Huh?"

"I know you've only been climbing a couple of weeks. Rob didn't say so, but word gets around. Just my luck to be stuck with a beginner."

So that was it! "Thanks," I said meekly. "I'll feel safe with an experienced climber belaying me."

We roped up, and I set off up the wall and promptly forgot everything—Rob, the Hare and the Tortoise, Trixie managing the rope down below, the other climbers . . . even Katie.

Rob had been right: the route was more challenging than any I'd attempted before. There were one or two slight overhangs, and a couple of places where the holds had been positioned far apart, so you really had to stretch. At one point I couldn't get my hand to the next hold, even at full stretch; the only way to reach it would be by doing a kind of leap upward and sideways. For the first time, I looked down to check that the belay rope didn't have too much slack, and that Trixie was concentrating. From the look on her face, I'd got the impression that my safety wasn't her prime concern. But she was keeping the rope at perfect tension and was watching me intently as I climbed. *Way to go, Trixie*, I thought, as I readied myself for the jump. *You may not be a fairy princess, but at least you take your belaying seriously.*

Time ceased to exist as I worked my way up that wall. Living moment by moment, hold by hold, breathing steady and even as I moved rhythmically up the rock, I knew again with a deep certainty that this was what I'd been born to do. All the bad-tempered Trixies in creation couldn't spoil it for me.

I reached the top, signaled, and was lowered smoothly down. I landed lightly on my feet, and couldn't help myself— I gave Trixie a huge grin of sheer delight.

To my utter amazement, she returned it with interest. The smile transformed her face—suddenly the glowering, troll-look vanished, replaced by a mischievous, irresistible charm. "If you're a beginner, I'm a two-headed gnu," she said. "Sorry I was bitchy before. It's just . . . I take my climbing seriously, and I thought . . ."

I knew what she'd thought: that I'd slow her down. I'd probably have felt the same, in her shoes. "No problem," I told her, "uh . . . Trixie."

She pulled a face. "I know . . . bummer of a name! Like some kind of Barbie doll or something. I must be the only kid saddled with a mum who'd name a child after a famous author—Beatrix Potter." I thought of my mum and old Charlie Dickens, and gave an inward grin. "I don't know which is worse—Beatrix or Trixie," she was rattling on, as she tied a figure-eight knot with nimble fingers. "When I get older, I'll probably change it legally, to Sarah or Jane or Gertrude or something—*anything* would be better than Beatrix."

"I see what you mean," I admitted. "It's a nice enough name, but it doesn't really suit you. Not that I know you, or anything. But you don't seem like a Trixie to me." I thought about myself; how I'd reinvented myself as Phil, and how just that one small thing made such a difference to how I saw myself—and how other people saw me. Not Pip, or Pippin, or Piphead, or Pipsqueak; but Phil. Phil McLeod. Maybe if I'd become Phil sooner, Katie would . . .

I pushed the thought of Katie out of my mind. Instantly, it was replaced by another. Before I could reconsider, I blurted it out to Trixie's back, poised to begin her ascent. "Hey," I said, "how about . . . *Beattie*? That fits better."

For a long moment she stood frozen, her back to me, considering. Then she turned and gave me a zillion-kilowatt beam. "I like it," she announced. "I like it a lot. *Beattie*." She held out her hand, square and firm and lightly powdered with chalk dust. "Here's to happy climbing, partner."

"Happy climbing, Beattie," I echoed, and we looked into each other's eyes and grinned.

The hour and a half passed in a flash, and before I knew it, we were walking out into the twilight together toward the bike rack. I'd had nothing to eat since lunch, and I felt a sudden pang of hunger. My hand reached into my pocket, where I often stashed leftover bits and pieces from my lunchbox—though it drove Mum crazy when she didn't remember to check, and bits of biscuit and sandwich crusts ended up in the washing machine.

My fingers encountered something firm and rectangular . . . something wrapped in smooth, crackly cellophane. I was still so befuddled from the climbing that I didn't remember what it was until I pulled it out: a giant licorice, pink and green and black, only slightly squashed by my climbing harness.

English had been the last lesson before break, on the last Friday of the term. Mrs. Holland had made us wait till the final ten minutes before she told us to put away our books and stand up and have a good stretch. Then, when we'd settled back at our desks again, she reached into her drawer and produced the bag of juggling balls.

An excited murmur rippled through the class. There were one or two groans. I felt a fluttering under my rib cage. "Now," Mrs. Holland was saying, "I wonder whether any of you remembered my challenge? Because *I* haven't forgotten—and I have ten snack-shop vouchers here, just waiting to be given out." She smiled at us, holding up a sheaf of pale green tokens. "Any takers?"

We looked around at one another sheepishly. No one wanted to be first, and I realized I didn't know whether anyone else had even made an effort to learn. Michael and I discussed it ages ago, with him bragging away about how he had a head start on everyone else. Even Katie had been dead keen, wanting to turn it into a personal duel between the two of us, in her usual way. But I had a funny feeling that today Katie wouldn't be up front with the juggling balls in her hands. She had other things on her mind.

"Come on . . . come on." Mrs. Holland was laughing. "Don't tell me none of you are even going to try? Twenty seconds is all it takes—twenty seconds, for a whole ten dollars to spend on rubbish to rot your teeth and hype you up for the rest of the day. Going once . . . going twice . . ."

Suddenly Mike jumped up and swaggered to the front of the class, grinning from ear to ear. And the floodgates opened—guys pushing back their chairs and joining him up at the front of the class, jostling and shoving and arguing about who was going to be first.

In the end, Mrs. Holland lined them up in alphabetical order, one behind the other. About ten guys had a go; no girls. Mike managed it—just. So did Paul. But the real surprise was Shaun, who'd questioned Mrs. Holland's own juggling ability. Shaun's surname is Wilson, so he got to go last. Everyone expected him to mess up, or fool around— Shaun has that kind of reputation. Not Mrs. Holland, though. She handed over the balls as serious as could be, and stood watching with a confident, approving smile. The entire class tittered—whatever Shaun was about to do, we knew from long experience it would be good entertainment value. The last thing anyone expected was for Shaun Wilson to juggle not three, but *four* balls in the air for thirty-five seconds on Mrs. Holland's stopwatch.

The entire class broke into applause. Shaun flushed and ducked his head and grinned. I figured maybe, like me, he thought it'd be pretty cool to do something hardly anyone else could—and do it well. He must have been practicing real hard, in deadly secret. In the space of thirty-five seconds, a lot of people's opinion of Shaun Wilson changed forever.

LICORICE

Mrs. Holland checked her watch. "Anyone else? There's a few more minutes to the bell. What about you girls? Going to let the boys outdo you? Surely not! Well then . . . Shaun, I think we'd all agree you've earned these." Shaun shuffled up to the front again, blushing like crazy, and shook Mrs. Holland's outstretched hand. Then he took the bag of juggling balls from her as if they were made of glass, and carried them back to his desk.

I expect you're wondering why I hadn't been there in line with the others. Truth is, I was wondering, too. I'd worked so hard to learn—surely the snack-shop voucher had been the whole point? Not just the voucher . . . the lure of winning those juggling balls, and saying good-bye to mandarins forever.

So what was stopping me?

Then suddenly, I knew. Shaun could have the juggling balls. Mrs. Holland was right: he'd earned them. For me, knowing I could juggle—and juggle well—was what really mattered. Knowing I'd achieved what I'd set out to do. And as for the juggling balls . . . well, I guess I'm just a mandarin guy at heart.

I was up in a flash, scooting out to the hallway where our bags were kept and digging in my lunchbox. Then I was standing in front of the class, my three mandarins—one slightly squashy, I noticed—in my hands. A wave of laughter ran through the classroom . . . but I didn't care. I glanced over at Mrs. Holland. "I didn't have any juggling balls, so I learned with these. They work just as well. Better, maybe."

At last, the class settled, and in the expectant silence I tossed first one, then two, then three mandarins up in the air . . . and juggled them for the entire two minutes till the bell rang.

Once we'd escaped from the crush at the snack shop, Mike and I retreated to our favorite haunt under the silver birch trees to gloat over our spoils. Mike had chosen a sherbet fizz and an arsenal of lethal gobstoppers. I'd eventually decided on an ice-cold can of ginger beer as well as my licorice, four for a dollar.

We finished our sandwiches first; then shared my mandarins. Next, I cracked open the ginger beer and sipped it, feeling the bubbles explode in my mouth and tickle the back of my nose. And then, at last, I took the cellophane off the first licorice, peeled apart the strips, and ate it slowly, bit by bit, savoring every morsel until it was all gone. It tasted just how I'd remembered. Better than the sandwich or the mandarins, that's for sure. Better than the ginger beer. Way better.

I'd kept two of the licorice in reserve. That's the way I am. I've still got Easter eggs dating back two years. Nick calls me a miser; Mum says I've got siege mentality, whatever that means. As for Dad, every year he growls that the Easter Bunny won't bother to come. But he says it with a twinkle in his eye, and he's never been right yet.

Now, outside the Igloo, listening to Beattie with half an ear, I unwrapped one of my last two licorice. It would be the perfect end to a perfect afternoon. Then, just as I was about to bite into it, I had a sudden thought. I dug in my pocket for the other. "Hey, Beattie—want one?"

"Oh—cool! They sell those at our school snack shop. But I'm not crazy about licorice, so it seems a waste to buy them."

"I don't usually. Today was what you might call . . . a special occasion. And I like the licorice part best." Carefully, I peeled them both apart—the green and pink filling for Beattie, slightly grimy from my fingers; the thin black strips of licorice for me.

Nibbling away, pushing our bikes side by side, and talking about climbing, we made our slow journey through the Igloo gate together, and off down the road.

NOMADS

It was Saturday—the first day of the winter holidays, and the last soccer match till the new term in two weeks' time.

Soccer was the one obstacle to get through before fourteen days of freedom—days I was planning to spend at the Igloo, making full use of the unlimited climbing pass Rob had given me the evening before. All the kids in the transition class were issued them for the holidays, though the others had to pay for theirs. Rob had passed mine over without comment; no one else had seen his quick grin and almost invisible wink.

We were playing a team called the Nomads, a good twenty-minute drive from home. We'd played them once before that season—they were based in Norton, practically out in the country. Last time, they'd won two-one. Dad had raged on the way home about their ref's timekeeping—according to him, she'd dragged the second half out for an extra five minutes to allow them to score the winning goal.

On the drive there, Dad was building the whole thing up

into a real grudge match. He'd had a bad week. The banana custard had sold like rat sandwiches, as Nick rather unwisely put it. Our fridge was crammed full of it, creeping steadily closer to its expiration date. Madeline loved it; Mum was nobly plowing her way through it; Nick had eaten one spoonful, announced it tasted like cat vomit, and been sent to his room in disgrace. As for me, each day I was taking a carton and tipping it down the toilet when no one was watching. One way or another, we were getting through it. But, as Dad rumbled when Mum cheerfully said so, that was hardly the point.

School holidays were always bad news for Dad. Heaps of people went away—but never us. What would happen if Dad's deliveries were suspended for a week, and people got in the habit of buying their milk somewhere else? The families who did go away put their deliveries on hold, and there were always some who never got around to taking them off again.

So today Dad's wrinkle barometer was set to *thundery and unstable—heads down*. He parked the truck and yanked on the handbrake. "Let's hope it's not that damn woman again," he muttered, reaching into the back for his parka. *Hang in there, Pip*, I told myself. *Just one match to go—half an hour each way, plus five minutes for oranges—and then there'll be no more Dad-soccer for two whole weeks! And once it starts again, it'll be more than halfway through the season!*

Dad's mood may have been black and threatening, but the weather wasn't. It was a perfect winter's day—fresh and crisp with a hint of ice in the air, a sky the color of a starling's egg, and the sun so bright it made you squint.

The other parents were exclaiming about the weather and comparing notes on their holiday plans. If this was a grudge match, it seemed to have passed them by. Dad gave me a squeeze on the shoulder that made me wince, grunted: "See you make a difference out there—this is one game we *have* to win!" and took up his usual position on the opposite side of the field.

Katie was concentrating on doing up her laces, ignoring me totally. Looking at my teammates' laughing faces, listening to them kidding around and watching them fooling with the ball, doing mock tackles and bragging about their dribbling skills, I wondered how it would feel to be them. To look forward to soccer every Saturday—to think of it as fun, as a game. To have the same flutter of excitement I felt about climbing as the time drew near for kickoff, instead of a gut-wrenching twist of nervous dread. If this was going to be a bad one, I just had to live through it. No big deal. It would soon be over.

Both teams took up their positions on the field. Jonathon and I were subbed off for the first ten minutes, so I kept my jacket on and hopped from foot to foot on the sidelines, trying to keep warm.

The game got off to a rip-roaring start. The Nomads were strong on attack and came close to scoring twice in the first five minutes; but, by some miracle, Katie and Mark got the ball away and up into the other half of the field. Not for long, though. We all knew it was only a matter of time before one of the shots peppering our goal went in. Sure enough, I caught a flash of the ball soaring into the top corner of the goalpost—the Nomads didn't have nets—and Tom leaping to save it in desperate spread-eagled silhouette. No go—our coach Andy, reffing the first half, blew a long, mournful blast on his whistle and our team regrouped, heads hanging low. One-nil to the Nomads.

Dad's voice rang out across the field: "*Def*ense! Come on, Colts, where's your *def*ense? They've got the measure of you—you'll have to do better than that! Let's see some positive play! Let's have a goal!"

Then Andy was signaling to me and Jon. We stripped off our jackets and jogged onto the field . . . and all I was aware of for the next twenty minutes was the thunder of feet and the thwack of the ball—with two more long blasts on Andy's whistle as the Nomads notched up another two goals.

I pretended not to notice Dad limping frantically up and down the sideline, pointing, shaking his fist, punching the air; yelling, yelling . . . always yelling.

At half-time we had a stern pep talk from Andy, and oranges. Despite the sweet, sticky juice dribbling down my chin, I had a sour, metallic taste in my mouth.

A couple of the other parents spoke to me the way they always did: with forced, cheery voices, as if I were deaf or very young. None of the other kids quite met my eye. I didn't look over at Dad. Couldn't.

All too soon the oranges were finished and their peels scattered on the grass. Andy took up his post beside our somber group of parents . . . and the Nomads coach marched onto the field to do duty for the second half. I felt nauseous. I wondered if I should tell Andy. Then maybe I could go home. Would Dad let me?

Never.

Their coach was the middle-aged mum of one of their players. If she'd ever played soccer herself, it was a long time ago, as Dad had pointed out sarcastically several times in the car—she had a wobbly butt in stretchy track pants, and her zip-up track top strained shut over a pot belly. But what she lacked in image, she made up for in attitude. Every strutting step she took, every shrill blast of the whistle, was a clear statement of her single-minded determination to win. She was a red flag to a bull.

The first few minutes of the second half passed in a blur. I was trying desperately to concentrate on the game, but it seemed all I could see was Dad hurrying up and down the sideline like a maniac, keeping pace with the play in a frantic limping shuffle. All I could hear was Dad, beside himself, yelling instructions to the team like a demented commentator. "*Pass! Pass* the ball, don't dribble, dammit! *Down the line! Yes!* Now—*shoot!* No, no, no—call that a shot? Colts—*get that ball!* Pip—*your ball!* Tackle, man—*tackle!*" On and on and on. I heard other things, too; things that made me wince and turn my face away. "*Shut him down! Take him out! Send him off!*"

The ref's face was set like granite. Every time she blew the whistle, it was with a sharper, angrier blast. I knew it was only a matter of time before she went over and spoke to Dad.

And then the ball came to me . . . and I was going for goal. This half, we were playing into the sun; it was hard to see the goal, and the Nomads' players were black shapes punched out of the brightness. But I didn't need to see—desperate to get a goal, to silence Dad's barrage of commands, I barged through them like a battering ram, ducking around some, shoving past others, leaping over a leg here, dodging a tackle there, fragmented flashes of startled faces strewn in my wake like shards of glass.

"Yes, Pip—*yes!* Go for goal! *Go all the way!* It's all yours! Now, Pip, *now—shoot!*"

There was another defender—the last between me and the goalie; he was coming in fast from the right—I didn't have a clear shot—*I didn't!* If I could just get 'round him, then—*then—*

"*Shoot*, dammit! *Now!*"

I broke stride, drew back my right foot, and shot with all my might, with all my pent-up misery and rage and shame. The ball met my foot sweet as a bell. It missed the defender by millimeters and blasted toward the goal mouth like a meteor. It was a high shot into the sun . . . but it was the shot of my life!

The goalie leapt for it, but he didn't even come close. The ball ricocheted off the crossbar in slow motion, almost invisible in the glare of the sun. A roar went up from our gaggle of parents. Andy's voice rang out, jubilant: "Great goal, Pip! Well done, Colts! Good try, goalie—bad luck!"

And from the other side of the field, Dad: "Pip! *Pip McLeod!* Go, Colts! *That'll show 'em!* One down—*three to go!* Now you've got 'em on the back foot! *Let's go!* We can still do it! *We can thrash 'em!*"

And that was when the ref blew her whistle—one long, officious blast—and shouted into the hubbub two words that somehow managed to be heard, and silenced everyone instantly—even Dad: "No goal."

"*No goal?*"

"Goal kick. The shot hit the crossbar."

"It hit the crossbar *and went in*!"

"It hit the crossbar and went over."

"*What?*"

"Take the goal kick. Play on!"

"Hold on one minute! That was a clear goal—you can't disallow it!"

"It was into the sun. The ball went over the bar, not under. End of discussion. *Play on.*"

For a second, I was afraid Dad was going to hit her. I could feel anger coming off him in waves so strong the vibrations reached me across the field and left me shaking.

But the Nomads' goalie had run and fetched the ball, and now he kicked it: a long, high kick that reached clear across to our side of the field and sent the players racing after it like a pack of greyhounds.

The game was underway again—the moment was past. For me; for the referee; for the other parents . . . but not for Dad.

NOMADS

When a shot of Mark's hammered into the Nomads' goal, dead center, right between the keeper's legs, Dad yelled out, "Better disallow it, Ref—seemed like it might have been *over the crossbar*."

The referee shot him a look that would have reduced most people to cinders . . . but not Dad.

For the next eternity, every decision the ref made was a chance for Dad to have another sarcastic dig. Even the parents watching the tenth-grade match on the other field were looking over and nudging each other and moving away. Then there was a scuffle and the ball rolled out over the sideline, close to where Dad was standing. The ref held up her hand: "Nomads' ball."

"Nomads' ball?" A disbelieving snort of laughter from Dad. "Oh *come on*, Tootsie! That's more than just incompetent, biased refereeing—that's blatant cheating! That ball came off a *Nomads'* player; it's a *Colts'* ball."

And that's when the referee marched right up to him, poked her finger in his face so close he blinked, and ordered him off the field. "Right—I've had enough of you, mister! Leave this ground, and leave it now!"

"Who the hell are you to tell me what to do? I'm staying right where I am. You don't own this field!"

"As the referee, I have a right to order anyone to leave who interferes with the course of the game. It says so in the rule book. And that's what I'm doing, right now! Leave the field *at once*!" And with that, she put the whistle to her lips and blew a single, shrill blast right in Dad's face.

There was a smattering of scattered applause from the Nomads' players. I watched as Dad's face slowly turned a blotchy purple. His eyes bulged, and his fists clenched.

Then I turned and walked quietly across the field, away from it all. I walked between the players as if I were invisible. No one even glanced at me. Every eye was fixed on the man on the sideline. I walked through the Nomads' goalpost as if it were the doorway into another world. I walked away across the grass, still crisp with frost in the places where the sun hadn't reached it yet. I walked past the line of parked cars; past Dad's truck, with the rust mark on the door where Mum scraped it at the supermarket; over the deep ruts its tires had made in the soft earth. I walked away down the deserted road, into the dazzle of the sun.

THE BALLOON BURSTS

I'd nearly reached the cluster of shops in the center of
Norton when I heard the rough roar of the truck's engine
coming up behind me. It skidded to a stop beside me. I
caught a glimpse of Dad's face. Looked quickly away.
Carried on walking.

I heard the truck lurch forward again; then Dad's door
burst open, and he was standing there in the middle of the
road glaring at me. "Where do you think you're going? What
the hell d'you think you're playing at? Get in the truck!"

I shook my head and walked on, not daring to look around.
I reached a junction; my soccer cleats make a clickety-clack
sound on the tarred surface as I crossed, like a little pony.

Dad's voice, from farther away, warningly: *"Philip . . ."*

I walked on. I heard the roar of an engine accelerating
and a screech of tires; then the truck angled untidily into a
parking place just ahead, and Dad slammed out and stormed
over to me, blocking my way. I'd never seen him so angry.

He stuck his finger in my face, rigid with rage. "You will

come with me right now. How *dare* you walk off the field in the middle of a match? What kind of behavior is that? Get in the truck *now*."

I felt dizzy. My heart was hammering; my knees were shaking so much I was scared I might fall. Dad loomed over me, huge and hulking, at the same time totally alien and utterly, heartbreakingly familiar.

A part of me—the Pip part, the part that would always be a little boy—longed to climb into the truck and say sorry and be forgiven. Another, stronger part of me was blazing with shame and anger—an anger more powerful than anything I'd ever felt. I looked Dad straight in the eye. "No."

Dad gaped at me. Stalemate. For an endless moment, we stood there, face to face. Then: "*How dare you defy me? How dare you humiliate me by walking off like that? No son of mine . . .*"

The balloon of anger inside me was swelling up now, threatening to burst. I felt it pushing at my chest, bulging up through my throat; it was making my ears ring, and squeezing hot tears out of my eyes. I clenched my mouth shut, blinked the tears away, and shoved past him. I'd taken two steps down the road when I felt his rough hand on my arm, spinning me around again.

"*No son of mine shames me in public!* Get in the truck before I throw you in! Don't you dare make a spectacle of yourself—or me. I'm warning you . . ."

And then the balloon burst.

"I'm not a son of yours!" I yelled. "*You hate me!* You're

ashamed of me! You only love Nick! Well, I've got news for you: *I hate you, too! I'm* ashamed of *you*—and how you rant and rave and carry on. Everyone's embarrassed to look at you! No one even wants to stand near you! I hate you, and I hate soccer! I wish you'd never come to a soccer match again! I hate you being there! I hate you and your green parka and your . . . your *bloody* truck! I'm walking home. *Leave me alone!*"

Dad was staring at me with a look on his face I'd never seen before.

I pushed past, knocking him out of my way with my shoulder, and stumbled down the road. I heard footsteps hurrying after me; felt a hand on my arm. "Pip . . ."

I spun to face him again. "*Don't touch me!* Let go of me! Stop trying to make me do stuff! Stop pushing me and shoving me in every direction that suits you! Stop trying to make me be different from how I really am! Stop trying to make me win everything and be best and—and *be like you*! I don't *want* to be like you! I just want to be me! But you won't let me! What are you trying to do? Are you trying to make me into how you were, before . . ."

Before the accident. Even as the other bitter words came pouring out of my mouth, as burning and unstoppable as hot jets of vomit . . . even then, I couldn't say it.

"It's not my fault! None of it's my fault! Why should I spend my life trying to make up for something that happened to you? You don't own me! You don't own my life, just because something wrecked yours!" I was crying now—

great, wrenching sobs that shook my whole body. I could sense a silent crowd gathering; people standing at a wary distance, watching, listening, their faces blank with shock. But all I could see was Dad, a dazed, baffled look on his face, something in his eyes . . .

Suddenly an image of that same face all those years ago flashed into my mind—when he'd just come out of the hospital, and the pain of his leg would make him close his eyes and sway. That was how he looked now. Tentatively, groping like a blind man, he reached out a hand again. "Pip . . ."

"*Leave me alone! Don't touch me!*" I yelled, tears streaming down my face.

Then I felt a gentle hand on my elbow; heard a hesitant, kindly voice in my ear: "Excuse me, son—do you need help? Is this man bothering you?"

Without turning around, without taking my eyes off that gray, stricken face, I answered: "Yes, he is. He's been bothering me all my life." Even to me, my voice sounded like a stranger's—flat, weary, adult. "He's my father."

THE FLOW

I turned and walked away—and this time, no one followed me. For a long time I walked blindly, propelled by anger and anguish—and by a peculiar, hollow feeling that had something to do with triumph, and something to do with shame. I walked all the way home, in a strange vacuum where time didn't exist.

There was no sign of the truck when I limped into our driveway. I registered its absence numbly.

Out of habit, I sat down on the step and untied my cleats. In an odd, detached way I noticed the studs were worn down to blunt nubs. It didn't matter. I'd never play soccer in them again. I was done with soccer. I was done with a lot of things. I peeled off my socks. Raw, angry blisters covered my feet.

"Pip—my little Pippin." It was Mum. "Your poor feet! What's happened, sweetheart? What's happened between you and Dad?"

"Where is he?" My voice came out a kind of croak.

"Out. Gone up into the mountains, I think. The way he does. When he needs . . . space."

Stiffly, I clambered up and headed for my room. Mum laid a tentative hand on my arm. "Pippin—if something's upset you both so much—you need to talk it through. Resolve it, however hard that seems. Things don't go away if you just ignore them."

I shook her hand off.

At the door, I stopped and looked back at her. Her eyes searched my face, but she didn't speak. "Ask him," I said flatly. "Ask Dad if you really want to know. Get him to *talk it through* . . . if you can."

Dad didn't come home for the rest of that day, and he didn't come home that night. There was a strange, empty feeling in the house, almost as though someone had died. Even Nick was subdued at dinner. I guess Mum must have said something to him beforehand, because he didn't mention Dad's empty place.

But one thing about Nick—he's not subtle, and he's not sensitive. I knew it wouldn't be long before he barged into my room wanting all the gory details.

I was sitting at my desk finishing my homework when my door creaked open and in he came. More and more, he seemed to be developing Dad's ability to fill up empty space with force and energy. Being around Dad and Nick always made me feel smaller, as if I had to kind of shrink into myself to make room for them.

But now, I slid off my chair and turned to face Nick, propping my butt on the edge of the desk and folding my arms across my chest. If Nick was going to get at the stuff on that desk—my stuff—he'd have to shift me out of the way . . . and I wouldn't make it easy.

Something of what I was feeling must have shown on my face because Nick gave me an uneasy sideways glance and hung around near the door, instead of breezing on in, in his usual way. "So, baby bro—what's up?"

"Nothing."

"Yeah, there is—I'm not dumb. Something's happened with you and Dad. You've done something to rile the old man." He waggled his eyebrows admiringly. "Something major, Pipsqueak. Howdja do it?"

"I don't want to talk about it."

"Aw, c'mon—I'm on your side, Pipsqueak. I'm just . . . curious."

"Well, you can stay curious. It's none of your business."

Nick rolled his eyes. "Jeez, Pipsqueak—what's got into you? Well, I guess I know when I'm not wanted." If he did, it was a first. I took a deep breath. Suddenly I felt like I was taking up just as much space as Nick was—maybe more.

"Close the door on your way out. Oh, and Nick—next time knock before you come in."

Nick gawked at me. *"Knock?"*

"You heard me."

"But you're just a kid, for crying out loud! Next thing you'll be telling me I should knock on Madeline's door!"

"I'm entitled to my privacy, same as you." I looked at him levelly. "Close the door on your way out."

Nick shuffled to the door, with one final, incredulous

glance over his shoulder. "No wonder Dad took off," he muttered. "Maybe I oughta join him."

But I wasn't finished. "And don't call me Pipsqueak. I don't like it. I never have."

Nick turned in the doorway, an expression of outraged innocence on his face, palms up in a gesture of surrender. "But it's just a nickname!" he protested. "It's . . . brotherly, you know? Affectionate!"

But it wasn't—and he knew it. *Pipsqueak* wasn't a nickname, it was a putdown. It was one of the strings Nick tweaked to make me jerk and twitch. Well, he wasn't going to manipulate me anymore. It had taken a lot of courage to get this far, and I wasn't backing down.

"It's not my name," I told him evenly.

We stared at each other across the room. Nick's dark eyes were narrowed, calculating; he knew, same as I did, that this was about more than just a nickname.

"We-ell, I dunno. Some habits are kinda hard to break . . . Pipsqueak."

"Think about it from my point of view. Just imagine if I had a nickname for you, an affectionate, brotherly nickname—and it slipped out by mistake—at school, say. In front of your friends. It might be embarrassing. Know what I mean . . . *Knickers?*"

Dad came home just after dark on Sunday evening.

We heard the sputter of the truck's engine, and its

headlights cut twin beams through the kitchen window as he turned in and parked. There was a long silence before we heard the car door slam and Dad's familiar, uneven footsteps come slowly into the house. In that silence, the whole house relaxed in one huge sigh.

Then Dad was in the kitchen doorway. He was wearing the faded camouflage pants he wears for hunting, and his green parka. His hair was rumpled, sticking up in rough black tufts, and he needed a shave. He had his rifle in one hand, and his battered old backpack in the other. He looked very tired.

He dropped the pack on the floor by the door, the way he always did. He looked over at Mum, and the wrinkles around his eyes deepened for a second. He glanced at Nick, briefly. He looked at Madeline, mangling her favorite cloth book in her highchair. His eyes rested on her like a caress. Instantly, she held out her arms to him. "Dada!" she shouted gleefully. "Uppy tiss!"

When he spoke, his voice was its usual gruff rumble. "I'm going for a shower. Milk run at five-thirty, same as usual." His eyes slid toward where I was standing, and away again without touching me. He turned, his wide shoulders filling the doorway, and limped away.

And that was how things were.

No mention was made of my outburst. As if it had never happened. No mention was made of soccer. I did the milk run with him, same as always. He was gruff, matter-of-fact, said little. Same as always.

Only one thing was different. Before, Dad had always looked me right in the eye, same as he did with everyone. I realized now it was part of the wrinkle barometer—the heart of it. When Dad's dark eyes looked into yours, you could read pleasure, amusement, warmth, anger, frustration—as clearly as reading words on a page.

Dad didn't look at me anymore. Oh, he *looked* at me, sure—but his eyes skidded off me as if I were made of ice. Skittered away like stones on a frozen puddle, before any contact could be made.

I wondered if this was how it was going to be forever. If it was, I was to blame—I knew that. That day in Norton, I'd smashed something that could never be mended. Except, like Mum said, by talking it through . . . and maybe not even then. But I'd discovered a deep-down part of me—a Dad-part, I suspected—that I'd never even known existed. A stubborn part. A part as cold and hard as metal, that wouldn't let me be first to back down.

Did Mum see it, too—did Nick? He was the same with them as always. And then one day toward the end of the holidays, Mum said something that surprised me.

"Your dad's a complicated man, Pippin," she announced out of the blue, walking past me with a freshly ironed pile of washing. "He seems like a real tough guy. And on the out-side, he is. But he's like one of those dipped ice creams—hard and brittle on the surface; soft as marshmallow inside. Deep down your dad's a real softie. Just like a little child."

THE FLOW

She smiled at me, her green eyes very warm and shining. Then she brushed past with her washing, leaving its sweet meadow fragrance hanging in the air.

To Nick and me, school holidays had always meant freedom—the freedom to go our own ways and do our own things, and those school holidays I lived and breathed climbing.

The second my bed was made, my room tidied, my breakfast eaten, and my chores done, I'd slip out of the house and zoom down the hill on my bike, the cold wind ruffling my hair and stinging my hands. With every heartbeat, my blood was singing: *climbing, climbing, climbing!*

Beattie and I stayed together as climbing partners. Within a day or two, I'd almost forgotten she was a girl—and completely forgotten I'd ever had any objection to her. She had a directness that made her just one of the guys—with Beattie, there were never any hidden agendas. WYSIWYG: What You See Is What You Get.

Pretty soon, everyone was calling her Beattie—even Rob. It was as if the grumpy troll called Trixie had never existed, and I'd been climbing with tough, offbeat Beattie, with her zany sense of humor and her cheeky pixie smile, forever.

She was a climbing partner in a million: the best belayer in the entire class. What's more, she shared my passion for climbing—for both of us, enough was never enough. When our muscles were creaking and our hands were raw, we'd look at each other and burst out laughing, our eyes locking in the unspoken question: *What's next?*

I learned more in those two weeks than I ever thought there was to know. The basic procedures surrounding equipment, knots, belaying and even leading became second nature, as easy as tying my shoes. And as that happened, it freed me to focus on the more technical, challenging aspects of climbing—the advanced techniques that separate the beginner from the true artist . . . the kind of climber I'd realized Rob was, and ached to be myself.

Rob left us much to our own devices—the climbing gym was like a giant playground where, so long as you knew the safety rules and stuck to them, the only limits were set by your own ability and ambition.

But every now and then, when we were grappling with what seemed an impassable overhang, or negotiating a series of holds that looked just plain unreachable, he'd materialize beside us—soft-spoken, always supportive, often humorous—to demonstrate a new hand grip or foot technique that made it all easy.

I developed a whole new vocabulary: heel hooks, edging, foot switches, bridging . . . and a whole lot more. Using carabiners and clipgates, quickdraws and Grigris became as simple as using a knife and fork.

I discovered the joy of taking on seemingly impossible challenges and overcoming them; of digging deep for reserves I never knew I had . . . then deeper still. Every now and then, I caught a glimpse in myself of the qualities that were so much a part of Rob . . . and of the kind of person I realized I wanted to be. Occasionally, when we stopped for a break or a drink of water, or to wolf down our sandwiches, Rob would wander over for a chat. "Of course you realize climbing is pure metaphysics," he'd say, his face serious but his eyes twinkling, so we were never sure whether he was teasing us. "Climbing isn't a sport; it's a religion. It isn't a recreation; it's a drug."

That part was true—I was addicted to the heady mix of power and balance, to the way every climb was a mind game, a challenge my brain took on in intimate partnership with my body.

As far as *metaphysics* was concerned, I stashed the word away in my memory bank, and looked it up in Mum's doorstopper of a dictionary when I got home. *Metaphysics*, it said: *the theoretical philosophy of being and knowing.*

Being and knowing . . . yeah, I reckoned Rob had that right, too.

The last Friday of the holidays, Rob set Beattie and me a special challenge. It was something he'd started doing a couple of days before—to keep us out of mischief, he said. He'd rig up a series of complex holds on an overhang, say; it would be ready and waiting for us when we arrived in the morning. "Go on then," he'd tell us with his crooked grin. "Let's see what you make of that. Red holds only—I'll check up on you in an hour or two." At first, we'd been so high on over-confidence and cockiness that we'd gone at it like bulls at a gate, certain we'd crack it within ten minutes, no problem. But Rob was as much of an artist at setting routes as he was at climbing them. What seemed simple from the ground would turn out to be agonizingly elusive ten meters up, dangling upside-down by your fingertips and toenails with your goal tickling your nostrils, as unreachable as the stars.

Every now and then, as we grappled with his latest creation, Rob would amble over, look up at whichever of us was climbing—or attempting to climb—and laugh. Most times that got the climber laughing, too—then you'd lose what grip you had and fall to the limit of the short anchor rope with a sickening jerk. Often, the shock of the fall would jolt out a word we'd never normally have dreamed of using . . . and that just made Rob laugh even more, and made us both even more determined that next time we'd do it for sure.

This Friday evening, we stayed on later than we meant to—do or die, we'd get up there before we left! I was so close—and then my precarious handhold slipped from my numb fingers and there I was, dangling from the rope cursing, while Beattie looked up at me and laughed. Grinning back down at her, checking my watch to see if we could squeeze in one more try each before we admitted defeat for the day, something drew my eye over to the main door leading to the rest of the Igloo.

There, standing in the shadows of the doorway, was a

tall, dark-haired figure in jeans and a sweatshirt. Standing, face expressionless, staring up at me as I swung on the end of my rope, as happy and at home as a chimp in a tree. Nick.

I'd completely forgotten Friday was the night he worked at the Igloo—completely forgotten my bike, a dead give-away in the bike stand.

I'd blown it.

THE POSTER

Knowing Nick, I guessed he'd wait till the following evening to drop his bombshell—till the whole family was together at dinner, and he could make his announcement with maximum impact. And knowing Nick, he'd expect me to search him out before then, and grovel, and see if I could negotiate some kind of a deal. It was exactly the sort of situation my big brother loved.

But I was just beginning to realize that, if I gave it a little thought, I could out-Nick Nick . . . maybe. So I stayed out of his way all Saturday, and slid into my place at the dinner table outwardly cool, hoping he couldn't see my heart thudding away under my sweatshirt.

Nick took his place opposite me, giving me an evil grin and a knowing wink. Every time he opened his mouth, even to take a bite of steak-and-kidney pie, my heart stopped. A couple of times, he wound me up deliberately. "Hey, Mum and Dad—you'll never guess who I saw at the Igloo yesterday evening!" Big bite of pie, chewing it properly for once instead of gulping it straight down like a python; enjoying keeping us all in suspense—me most of all. His black eyes sparkling with malicious enjoyment as they rested on me, hoping I'd squirm. Then, eventually: "Mr. Wood—Katie's dad. In a brand new tracksuit, heading for the gym. What's got into the old fart, d'you think?"

I ate my way steadily through my pie, ignoring him, concentrating on separating out the kidney. In the old days, Dad would've reached over and scraped it all onto his plate before I'd finished, without so much as a "please." But now the little pile of kidney lay slowly congealing on the side of my plate.

After dinner, there was a knock on my door.

"Come in, Mum," I called.

But it wasn't Mum. It was Nick. He closed the door behind him and leaned against it, arms folded, a smirk on his face. But it was a different smirk from usual—for once, he seemed slightly unsure of his ground. "So, Pipsqu—Pip," said Nick. "Looks like I've found out your secret, huh?"

"Secret?" I echoed innocently. "What secret?"

"You've been sneaking off to the Igloo, hanging out at that Climbing Center, without telling Mum and Dad! For how long? And where've you been getting the money? If Dad knew . . ." He let the sentence hang in the air unfinished, whistling softly and shaking his head.

I shrugged.

"I could tell, you know." He shot me a calculating look from under his dark brows.

"Yep. You could."

Nick frowned. "Dad'd go batshit."

I shrugged again. "Maybe."

"Don't you . . . *care*?"

"Not much. I'm not doing anything wrong. If Dad doesn't like it, that's his problem." At least, that was how I'd tried to justify it, lying awake in the middle of the night, wondering what would happen when Mum and Dad found out. Because eventually, they would. Now, hearing myself saying the words to Nick, they sounded shallow and full of bravado . . . to me, at any rate.

But not to Nick, apparently. He gave me a sudden grin—almost like a friend instead of a big brother. "Tough talk," he said. "I can see why you don't want him there, bellowing out instructions from the bottom of the wall. Good old Dad—he'd be enough to make you fall for sure!" He crossed the room and grasped me by the shoulders, looking seriously into my eyes. "So your secret's safe with me. For now. But remember: you owe me, big time."

At the door, he turned back, like he always did. Nick can never leave a room without delivering a parting shot. Wearily, I looked up from my book again. "What now?"

There was a funny smile on his face—a smile I hadn't seen for years, not since we were little boys. When he spoke, his voice was deliberately casual. "I was just wondering—it must be pretty hard, that climbing stuff. Scary. You were way high, man." He frowned, and seemed to hesitate. I waited, keeping the place in my book with my finger. "You made it look easy, bro. Way to go, Pip."

THE POSTER

School started again. I spent the whole of that first week feeling like one of those Roman galley slaves chained to the bench to stop them from rushing off and leaping overboard to freedom. Friday and climbing seemed light years away.

As for Katie, she acted like a stranger. I'd hardly seen her during the holidays—just her back view in the Woods' garden once or twice, and a glimpse of her profile in their car, disappearing around the corner. It looked as if we'd moved on to a new equation: a C-type relationship. One that didn't exist.

On Thursday, Mum tapped on my bedroom door and popped her head 'round. "Pippin—about soccer on Saturday. Dad says I'll be taking you from now on."

My heart gave a sudden, painful little lurch. I'd been wondering what would happen about soccer. Now I knew. *You feel relieved*, my brain told me. *You've got what you wanted!*

I guess so. Yeah. That must be what I'm feeling. Relief.

I realized Mum was still standing at the door, waiting for me to say something. "Uh—yeah. Okay," I mumbled.

She waited a long moment more, giving me one of those Mum-looks that are like X-rays—the ones that see through everything. Then she left without saying another word, closing the door quietly behind her.

Walking into the climbing gym on Friday, I felt like a fish that's been flapping around on dry ground slowly suffocating and suddenly flops back into the water . . . and hey—it can breathe again and zooms away with a flick of its tail! Beattie's face lit up like a sparkler when she saw me; she swaggered over, already in her harness, and gave me a high-five—and then a hug that just about busted my rib cage.

The hour and a half climbing session seemed to last about ten seconds.

Beattie had to leave early—it was her mum's birthday, and she and her dad were planning a special surprise birthday dinner. "A shock, more like," Beattie told me wryly. "Dad can't cook for peanuts, and neither can I—but it's the thought that counts, he reckons. If we poison poor Mum in the process, it's irrelevant—or so Dad says. Try telling *that* to the coroner!" I grinned to myself. Somehow it didn't surprise me that Beattie wasn't the domestic type. I'd have loved to be a fly on the wall but, knowing Beattie, she'd give me a blow-by-blow description next week, suitably exaggerated.

Rob belayed me for the final five minutes—we'd been trying a new route aptly named Nutcracker, way harder than any we'd ever attempted before. By the time I'd changed shoes and stashed my gear in the locker, the gym was deserted. Normally I'd have said good-bye to Rob, but he didn't seem to be anywhere around. I walked to the door, and out into the passageway that led to the rest of the Igloo.

THE POSTER

And there was Rob, pinning a poster onto the notice board beside the door.

Highlands Regional Sport-Climbing Championships, it said in huge letters across the top.

If the entire Igloo had suddenly lifted off and gone into orbit, I wouldn't have noticed. I stared at that poster, the words lodging in my brain one after the other like cold lead bullets. *Hey! Bet you could do really well in that!* my brain squawked excitedly.

Shut up! Butt out! Leave me alone! Don't you understand anything? *I've had enough of all that win, win, win stuff to last me a lifetime!*

"It's in just over a month's time, on the Friday of the long weekend." Rob's voice seemed to be coming from far away. I tore my eyes from the poster and looked over at him. He was pushing the last pin into the top corner of a blank sheet headed *Registration: Climbing Championships*. "We're holding it here this year."

Without meaning to, I was slowly backing away from the poster; away from Rob. "I . . . I think we might be going away that weekend."

"I hope not. Actually, I'm glad to have you on your own for a sec—I've been wanting to talk to you about which category would be best for you to enter."

So here it was again. Here, in the Igloo, the Climbing Center, the one place I'd thought I was safe. Coming from the one person I'd thought I could trust. He was smiling down at me, his blue eyes twinkling like someone offering some kind of wonderful treat.

I took a deep breath. "I'm not going to enter," I mumbled, staring down at my scuffed old sneakers. "I'm not interested. I—I don't want to . . . to . . ." *To turn climbing into what soccer's always been. A vehicle for competition, a platform for failure.* But how could I ever begin to explain that to Rob? Despair fell over me like a shadow, as if the sun had disappeared behind a bank of thick gray clouds. I'd truly believed climbing was different. I'd truly believed Rob was different. But I'd been wrong—on both counts.

Rob was giving me his familiar crooked grin. "Don't worry, Phil," he said cheerfully. "You're more than ready for this. You'll do great—it'll be fun. I know you haven't been climbing long, but—"

I felt betrayed.

"Will you listen to me? I don't want to enter. Competitions and stuff—I'm not into it all!" I'd started off sounding real calm and reasonable . . . but with every word, I could feel pain and frustration building inside me like a giant wave. Part of me was scared of where that wave was sweeping me—but it was already too late. Without meaning to—without wanting to—I could hear myself starting to talk louder and louder, till I was almost shouting. "*I don't want to enter!* I won't—and you can't make me! Climbing's something I do for *me*! Not for you, or . . ."—*or Dad*—"or anyone else! I don't *care* about competitions! I'm not interested in winning and losing, and championships, and—and . . ."—a word the bookish

kids at school were constantly using surfaced in my mind—
"*rankings*, and all that *crap*! I don't want any part of it! I
won't be forced into it! I won't be pressured and pushed and
bullied and yelled at and expected to win! You can pressure
someone else! I'll give up climbing if it gets to be like that!
You can't make me, and neither can anyone else!"

I was yelling at him now, my voice echoing in the bleak
corridor, my hands clenched into fists and—I realized to my
horror—scalding tears on my cheeks. I was yelling at Rob,
but his wasn't the face I was seeing. I squeezed my eyes shut
and took a deep, shuddering breath, half afraid of what
would come out next. But I needn't have worried. Instead of
words, a storm of hiccupping sobs tore out of me . . . I
turned my face away, shoved past him, and ran for the sanctuary of the sheltering dark.

My hands were shaking so much when I reached my bike
that I couldn't get the combination right on the lock—couldn't
see it clearly enough in the darkness, through my tears. A fine,
misty rain was falling, making the lock feel greasy and my fumbling fingers slip. I was sobbing like a baby, desperate to get
away. I never wanted to see Rob again. I didn't want to see the
look I knew would be on his face . . . the look I'd seen so often
on Dad's. Disappointment.

When I left the Igloo—when finally my numb fingers
managed to undo the lock and I could ride away—I knew
I'd never come back. It would be another ending, another
good-bye. At long last the two halves of the lock fell apart . . .
and at the same moment, a voice spoke softly behind me.

"Phil. Hey—turn around and look at me." Fiercely, I knuckled the tears away. I didn't want to turn—didn't want him to know I'd been crying. *Boys don't cry.* But the kindness in his voice told me he already knew. And it didn't matter.

Slowly, very slowly, I found myself turning to face him. He was smiling down at me—that familiar smile, with the ironic twist at the corner. "Phil—that conversation we just had, back there. I have the weirdest feeling I missed part of it." My nose was running. I wiped it on the back of my hand and sniffed. And listened. "The part where I said you *had* to enter the Climbing Championships. The part where I said I expected you to win—or do well—expected you to do *anything*, in fact. I don't know who's pressuring you, kid, but one thing I can promise: it isn't me. Okay?"

I nodded dumbly, my head spinning, a gaggle of remembered words and fragments of sentences scrolling through my brain. Rob was talking again, his real words overlaying the imagined ones with an urgency I'd never heard from him before. "I've been where you are now. I look at you and I see myself ten-odd years ago, playing dodge ball with things only I could see. I know what I was running from when I was your age. But with you, it's something different. I don't know what—don't want to know. I know what I see, though. I see a kid who comes to the gym and climbs like an angel, with no one ever there to watch him. And I wonder why. I see a kid who's using climbing to get away from something, as fast as he can go. Something . . . or someone. And I have the feeling that someone may not be who you think it is. I've been there, too. Been there; done that. Got the T-shirt . . . and the scars."

I drew in a long, shaky breath. "I have to go home," I muttered.

Raindrops shone like tiny diamonds among the untidy strands of hair framing Rob's face. His skin glistened, slick with rain, but he didn't seem to care. "Hang on a sec, Phil—hear me out. That heavy stuff is part of growing up—the painful part. The other issue's a lot simpler. So, you have strong feelings about competition. I don't know where they come from, but one thing's for sure: they're valid. You're right. Competitive sport can be hell. Approached the wrong way, there's only ever going to be one winner—one out of a million or two, and all the rest losers. And even that one guy won't win forever.

"But sport doesn't have to be like that, Phil. Think about it. Who are you really competing against? Not just in climbing—in any sport? Once you've got that figured out, you'll realize that everyone can be a winner. In sports . . . and in life."

His face looked distracted in the watery moonlight. I had a sense that he'd been talking to himself as much as to me. Then he grinned—a grin warm with humor—and pushed the damp tangle of hair back off his forehead. "You look how I feel: like a drowned rat. You need to get on home, kid. And so do I. We're having friends 'round and I promised I'd give Chris a hand with dinner.

"Before you head off, though: about the Championships. Enter or not, it's up to you. Either way, it's cool with me. And I mean that. Just one thing, though. Whatever you do, do for yourself—and remember: there's no such thing as failure."

THE FOURTH MANDARIN

I rode home. Did the milk run with Dad. Ate dinner. Went to bed. Played soccer the next morning, with Mum and Madeline socializing on the sidelines. Came home. Had lunch. I did all of it on autopilot.

I needed to think. I needed to be alone to focus my mind on what Rob had talked about. What had he meant—I was using climbing to get away from something? That was crazy! I climbed because I enjoyed it. Enjoyed it, and was good at it. Really good. But was there more? Deep down, in my most secret heart? Did I want to get something more out of my climbing—to test myself, see how good I *really* was? Or was I happy just to scuttle up and down walls for the rest of my life, like a rat on a treadmill?

I didn't even begin to know. That was how my thoughts felt—as if they were on a treadmill, going 'round and 'round in circles, getting nowhere. 'Round and 'round in circles . . . up and down and 'round and 'round, in an endless cascade.

Scooping a double handful of mandarins out of the fruit

bowl, I headed for my room. Madeline trundled hopefully after me, but I closed the door firmly behind me. "Sorry, Madeline—not right now. I need to be on my own for a while."

I could juggle three mandarins now without even thinking about it—the rhythm had become as natural as breathing. For weeks now, I'd been juggling everything I could lay my hands on—pencil sharpeners and erasers at school; Madeline's toys; socks; apples—I'd even had a go with some eggs, just quickly, when Mum was safely out in the garden. But nothing beat mandarins.

For a while I stood at the window, juggling, feeling my tangled thoughts unfurl and smooth out and flutter away across the valley like ribbons. Across the valley . . . to where the Igloo gleamed white in the afternoon sun. Juggling and climbing . . . were they really so different?

I'd started juggling because of Mrs. Holland, and for the licorice . . . but most of all, because it was something I knew I could do well, if I put my mind to it. The challenge had been to juggle three balls. I'd achieved it; and that was where I'd left it. But was it really enough? Why stop at three? Why not go on to four, like Shaun Wilson? Or maybe even five, like Mrs. Holland? Come to think of it, three was getting kind of boring.

I looked down at my bed. There, looking about as smug as it's possible for an orange to look, lay the fourth mandarin . . . as if it had known it'd be needed, all along.

I soon discovered juggling four mandarins is a trick. Sure, all juggling's a trick, but four mandarins is a special trick. A trick of the eye, an optical illusion. It said so in my book. When you juggle four balls you're really juggling two columns of two balls, each in a separate hand. Watching, you think they cross over; but really, they never do.

That whole weekend, every spare minute I had, I concentrated on juggling. First, I perfected two mandarins with my dominant left hand—the easy one. Then I worked on the right hand. It was harder, but I kept practicing until it was every bit as good as the left. Then, late Sunday afternoon, I put the whole thing together. It was kind of like patting your head and rubbing your stomach at the same time—but I guess all juggling's like that, when it comes down to it. By bedtime, I was juggling four mandarins perfectly. I could have carried on all night. The entire weekend had flown past without me thinking about Rob or the climbing competition, even once.

When I woke up on Monday morning, I realized I hadn't needed to think about it. The decision was made.

The Igloo had a different feel from its usual Friday bustle. There was a scatter of cars in the parking lot; two middle-aged guys in baggy track pants and sweat-stained T-shirts were chatting at the entrance, and a harassed-looking mum was hustling two reluctant toddlers along, obviously headed for a lesson at the swim center.

I didn't even know if Rob was there on Monday afternoons. In a way, I hoped he wasn't. I wasn't planning on speaking to him—not today. I'd made up my mind what I was going to do. Now I just had to do it.

I dug in my book bag for a pen and padded softly through the main arena toward the Climbing Center. For once, no games were in progress on the indoor courts—the whole place had a silent, spooky feel, like a ghost town.

As I neared the familiar corridor, it was as if all those times I'd been there before had somehow melted away and I was in a kind of time warp, back to the very first time I'd ever been inside the Igloo. I felt like a trespasser— an intruder.

The corridor was deserted, silent except for the faint hum of the air conditioning. The poster was still there, with the registration list beside it. Someone had drawn a mustache on the girl in the picture. A couple of names were up already. There were columns, I saw now: Boys 14 and Under; Boys 18 and Under; with the same for girls. Male Open. Female Open.

What had Rob said? *I've been wanting to talk to you about which category would be best for you to enter.* Well, I was thirteen. Simple enough.

But then, just as I was about to start writing, a name leapt off the sheet at me, practically punching me in the face. Most of the names had been printed in blue ballpoint, using the pen dangling from a string next to the list. But this one was in bold black rollerball, untidily scrawled over two lines. *Jordan Archer.* It was in the column headed "Boys 18 and Under."

Without stopping to think I wrote my name right

underneath, in my small, neat handwriting, keeping carefully to the line. *Phil McLeod*.

Then I took a step back and looked at what I'd done. There was nothing I could do about it now, other than cross it out. And I wasn't about to do that.

Mum had made chocolate cake. I wolfed down two massive slices, and Madeline kept me company, smearing most of hers over her face. I cleaned her up and, while I did, I explained to her how important it is to do things for yourself, because you want to, and not for someone else. Even walking. And I told her how she must never, ever be afraid to fail. She took it all in stride, the way she does.

Then I laid a neat little trail of raisins all down the length of the sofa. I positioned her carefully at one end, and watched proudly as she shuffled her crab-like way down the line, hanging on, snaffling each one up as she got to it.

For a second, I found myself starting to worry about her technique. What if I were letting her get into bad habits? But then I figured, *So what? If she ends up only ever walking sideways, who cares? She'll get where she's going just the same. And that's all that really matters.*

BEING AND KNOWING

"So." Rob gave a quick glance up from the tangle of cara-biners he was sorting, and then down again. "You signed up, huh?"

I looked down, pretending to check my figure-eight knot. "Yeah." *I made up my own mind*, I wanted to tell him. *And I'm doing it for me, like you said. But I'd still give anything to know what you think.*

"Did I enter the right age group?" I asked instead.

He turned away and hung the carabiners on their special rod in the locker. When he turned back, there was a broad grin on his face. "You entered the category that'll give you the most challenge, that's for sure," he said. "You'll be up against kids three, even four years older than you, with a height advantage, a reach advantage, a strength advantage . . . and years more climbing experience. You'll be head-to-head with some of the top climbers in Highlands, who know the ropes—literally—back to front and inside out, and have entered more climbing competitions than you've had hot breakfasts."

I blinked. He wasn't being very encouraging.

"But that won't bother you," he carried on breezily, "seeing as you're not in it to win. Right, Phil?"

"Uh—yeah, right," I mumbled. "Though . . ."

"Though?"

I stumbled on, feeling like I was about to trip over my own feet. "Though . . . I don't want to . . . like . . . make a total fool of myself. If I'm entering, I want to do the best I can. If there's anything I can do between now and then that will help me climb faster, or higher, or better—well, I want to do it. Will you help me?"

"Of course I will. That's what I'm here for. First, though, you need to know what you've got yourself into. Do you know what an on-sight leading competition is?"

"I know what leading is," I ventured.

"Yeah, that's part of it. You'll be leading—placing running belays, clipping yourself onto the wall—as you climb, with a belayer down below. But there's more to it than that. There are heaps of different kinds of climbing competitions: bouldering, redpointing, speed climbing . . . even ice climbing. But on-sight leading is by far the best measure of a climber's true ability—which is why we've chosen it for the older climbers.

"It's pretty simple. There'll be three rounds, each more difficult than the last. You're scored on the height you reach in each round, with only the best scores advancing to the next. At the end there's a final—a few evenly matched climbers, pitting their skills against the most challenging route. Whoever gets highest on that is the overall winner."

In spite of myself, I liked what I was hearing. The routes would be tough, and I had to admit that knowing I'd be up against other climbers . . . well, it would make me try that extra bit harder. Whether I liked it or not, it was a fact.

"Just one other thing," Rob continued casually. "The *on-sight* part means you'll be climbing routes you've never seen before. You get six minutes to preview each route with the other competitors and plan your strategy—visualize sequences; check out the holds—you know the drill. You've been doing it subconsciously ever since you first walked in here. Then you're all taken to an isolation area, to prevent you from discussing the route with your coach or anyone who's already climbed. You climb one at a time; then you move across to the viewing area and watch with the spectators." He shrugged. "And that's pretty much it. Sound like fun?"

Fun? It sounded terrifying! Terrifying—and thrilling. I nodded. The questions crowding my mind had jostled themselves into a kind of log jam—not a single word could find its way out past the enormous grin plastered all over my face.

Rob looked down at me, eyes narrowed, considering. And then, at last, he said what I'd been waiting to hear. "One look at your face tells me you've made the right decision. You're doing the right thing, for the right reasons. Seems to me you're climbing *toward* something now—and I'll do all I can to help you get there."

The month before the Climbing Championships flashed by like an express train. One day followed another in a blur of school, homework, milk run, chores—as few as I could get away with—soccer . . . and training.

"The best way to improve your climbing is by *climbing*," Rob had told me. "No surprises there. You can't get to the Igloo as often as you'd like, but there are other things you can do to give you the edge. Work on your basic fitness by staying active—no problem for a guy your age. It's good that you bike to school; even better that you live on the hill. Your build is a huge advantage. Skinny rock spiders like you and me make great climbers—less blubber to lug up the wall."

Together, we worked out a simple training schedule I could do in my room at home, in private. In secret—though I didn't tell Rob that. First, a warm-up routine Rob made me swear to stick to like glue, followed by ten minutes a day of sit-ups, push-ups, and strengthening exercises for my feet and calves. Systematically stretching every single muscle in my body. Squeezing the old squash ball I'd unearthed from the toy closet, first in one hand, then in the other, for as long as I could. Rob suggested I find somewhere to rig a pull-up bar—and the old tree behind the garage had a horizontal branch at just the right height. It was hidden from the house, too—an added bonus.

"Mental training is the most important," Rob told me.

"I've seen countless climbers bomb out because of mental attitude. They were afraid they'd fall. So they fell—no surprise. They were worried about a particular obstacle on the climb; sure enough, they couldn't get past it. Ever heard of visualization? For a climber, it's the ability to see yourself at the top of that wall. Once you can do that, you're there. Believing in success will make it happen, every time."

There was another part of my training I didn't tell Rob about. It had to do with balance, timing, rhythm, focus—all the things Rob talked about, not just in relation to climbing, but as part of his philosophy of life.

Juggling.

And in my own mind, as I deftly juggled two, three, and four mandarins and struggled in vain to master five, I repeated three words over and over in my mind. Like a magic formula . . . almost like a prayer. *Being and knowing. Being and knowing. Being and knowing.*

All that training, and Mum and Dad didn't suspect a thing. As for Nick, he kept his word not to tell—and, anyhow, he was too busy with the build-up to his final zone trial to think about anything else. While I was living and breathing climbing, Nick was living and breathing soccer.

And Katie . . . well, who knew? One thing was for sure: she was changing. Nothing you could put your finger on; but that old, tomboyish matter-of-factness seemed to be peeling away like a dry, old snake skin. Beneath it a silky, sinuous, even more beautiful Katie was emerging—one I knew in my heart would always be a stranger to me.

BEING AND KNOWING

Those first days, I'd watched her from the corner of my eye, my heart skipping a beat if she turned toward me or looked like she were walking over. But it never happened.

Gradually, I found I was avoiding her, too—not consciously, but just kind of choosing to be where she wasn't. By the time the climbing competition rolled around, I'd pretty much forgotten she even existed.

GUMBY

Friday—a public holiday. The day of the Climbing Championships . . . but only I knew that. The day of Nick's final Junior Youth zone trial. The whole world knew *that*— he'd been talking about nothing else for weeks.

Most days, our family had breakfast on the run. It was usually a bowl of cereal gobbled while we finished our homework at the kitchen table, milk dribbling down our chins, or a slice of toast crunched while we unearthed our clean gym gear from the laundry basket, scattering crumbs on Mum's fresh washing. Sometimes it might be an apple or a banana finished as we swooped down the hill on our bikes.

Not today, though—not the day of Nick's soccer trial. Today, we all sat down at the kitchen table for breakfast. "I need to have baked beans before my big trial, Mum," Nick had announced a couple of days before.

Beans, beans, musical fruit:
The more you eat, the more you toot;
The more you toot the better you feel—
So eat baked beans for every meal!

"Nicholas . . ." growled Dad warningly.

"Seriously, though," Nick backtracked hastily, "baked beans are way the best—no fat; practically pure carbohydrate. I should have baked beans for breakfast . . . and jelly beans to give me instant energy at half-time."

"Jelly beans?" roared Dad, his eyebrows practically disappearing into his hairline. "What happened to oranges? What was good enough for me is good enough for you, zone trials or no zone trials."

Nick's never one to give up easily. He treated Dad to a long lecture on the glucose-accessibility of jelly beans versus every other known food form, and cited the Soccer Federation and even the great Ivan Kingsley himself as the source of this dietary breakthrough. Believe it or not, it was true—even our low-tech coach, Andy, had muttered something about it at soccer practice. But, unfortunately for Nick, he'd cried "wolf" too often. Dad wasn't buying it—and he certainly wasn't buying jelly beans.

Nick did get his baked beans, though. I'd been doing some reading on nutrition, and I figured what was true for Nick was true for me. "Can I have baked beans, too?" I asked Mum, watching as she ladled the first steaming spoonful onto Nick's plate.

"Oh, Pippin—there aren't enough for both of you, I'm afraid—there's only one tin. Nick needs a good breakfast, today of all days. How about some toast? There's a scraping of honey left in the jar."

Madeline was also on the baked-bean trail.

"Dis!" she demanded. "Me dis!"

Mum stopped in mid-ladle, looking helplessly around at all the faces turned to the stove, all eyes fixed hopefully on the single tin of baked beans. "I wish there were enough for all of you," she said quietly.

"Life's tough," said Nick with a wolfish grin. "Give, Ma."

Then a gruff voice spoke up from behind the newspaper. "Divide the tin between them, Trish. In this family, we share what we have. Anyone who's still hungry can fill up on toast. That's carbohydrate, too, hotshot."

Dad? I couldn't believe it! I looked over at him in astonishment, but he was invisible behind the sports page. I shot a glance at Nick. He was scowling with fury; but even he knew that he could kiss his remaining baked beans good-bye if he argued. Without a word, Mum set a plate down in front of my brother, then me, then a bunny plate with a few beans in front of Madeline. As she passed Dad, she rested her hand for a moment on his shoulder—just the gentlest touch.

"Hot-bot! Hot-bot!" Madeline chanted, smearing patterns in the tomato sauce with her fingers and trying to wedge a bean up her nose. As for me, I ate every scrap. They tasted great. I would've licked the plate, if I hadn't known from experience that Dad's eyes could see through a zillion layers of newspaper.

As the dust was settling after Dad and Nick's departure and I was unobtrusively getting together some provisions for the day ahead, Mum came over and put her arm around me. "I've been thinking, Pippin: it's a glorious day. Why don't the

three of us do something together—go to the aquarium, perhaps; then have a picnic in the park. What do you say? We
hardly seem to see you these days."

I goggled at her, aghast. "But, Mum . . . I . . . uh . . ."
There was no way I could risk telling her. Mum was cool—
but Mum shared everything with Dad. What I told her, I'd
be telling him. But I didn't want to lie. "I'm sorry, but I've
already planned something."

She looked at me searchingly. "Pippin—you're not getting
into any kind of trouble, are you? Every time I turn around
you're sloping off to your room . . . late back from school . . .
the whole holidays, we hardly saw you. Is it Dad? Is it this
thing with Dad . . . ?"

I pulled away. "Aw, Mu-*um*. It's not a *thing* with
anyone—and of course I'm not in any trouble. I just . . . I just
have my own friends, and . . . and stuff to do." I shot her a
wary glance to see how she was taking it. She was wiping
down Madeline's little table, over and over again—though it
looked clean enough to me.

I went over and gave her a one-armed hug—the kind of
hug that pulls close and holds away at the same time; the
kind of hug that means *I'm sorry . . . and I'm not. I love
you . . . but keep your distance.*

Then I threw my gear into my school bag and headed off
down the hill to the Climbing Championships.

Turning in through the gates, I saw the big parking lot
was already nearly full. **Highlands Regional Sport-Climbing
Championships**, announced the electronic billboard. I felt a

twinge of nerves, even though I wouldn't be competing until the afternoon.

Everywhere, families were hurrying toward the entrance—kids in warm-up gear and tracksuits, loose pants and sweatshirts, some swinging their own harnesses, some with gear bags . . . even one or two with helmets. Dads lugged cooler boxes; mums carried armloads of jackets and hampers of picnic stuff.

The cycle racks were already full. I propped my bike against the Igloo wall and clicked on the lock. Then I shouldered my bag and strode through the big double doors, trying to look confident. But suddenly I felt very alone—as isolated as if I were stranded on some desert island, in spite of all the people jostling me and the babble of voices.

Then I was pushing my way down the passage and into the climbing gym . . . Rob was waving to me across the room and giving me a thumbs-up . . . Beattie was grabbing me by the hand and dragging me across to the registration desk, jabbering away like a tape on fast forward. And from then on, it was all action. I'd put my name down to help with the belaying for the junior classes during the morning, and it kept me so busy it seemed like I'd hardly arrived before we were breaking for lunch. I struggled to force down a honey sandwich and a banana while Beattie—who'd walked away with first place in the Under 14 Girls—pointed out my major opposition in the Under 18s.

Beattie's one of those people who always seem to know everyone and everything. "See that tall guy over there—the one with the dreadlocks?" she hissed in my ear through a mouthful of chocolate brownie. "He's Troy Gilmour, captain of the Highlands climbing team. He's too cool even to wear his team tracksuit—oh, swoon!" Sarcastic as only Beattie can be. "And over there—look—that's Jordan Archer. He would've made the team last season if there hadn't been some kind of an objection, or technical incident, or something . . . reckon he fancies himself or what? I guess he *is* rather a hunk, though I hate to admit it. That must be his girlfriend—the soccer star. Selected for the zone team at the Under 14 trials last weekend, though I must say she doesn't look like a soccer player to me! And that's Jordan's coach next to him. Technically one of the best in the country, and a real slave-driver. His sportsmanship's a bit suspect, though. Win or bust, and heaven help you if you get in his way. Suits Jordan, though, I'll bet. Two of a kind. And over by that wall—at the bottom of Climb Thirteen . . ." But I'd stopped listening. I couldn't tear my eyes away from Jordan and Katie.

Most of the climbers—even the legendary Troy Gilmour— wore loose-fitting pants and track tops or sweatshirts. They were wearing the stuff they were planning to climb in underneath, like me—my most comfortable pair of skuzzy old shorts and my lucky green T-shirt with the holes under the arms.

Not Jordan. He was broadcasting his status as a serious climber loud and clear. He had on tight-fitting, electric-blue climbing pants, like those tights ballet dancers wear. They showed off his trim waist and muscular thighs, every single muscle in his butt . . . and a lot more besides. A loose-fitting designer T-shirt looked like it had been hacked off with a chainsaw just above belly-button level in a carefully judged "don't give a damn" statement, and a show-off designer gear bag was slung casually over one shoulder. He was deep in conversation with his coach, a compact, muscular man with a grim, intense expression that reminded me of Dad. While he talked, Jordan gestured with one hand; brushed his dark red—*auburn*—hair back from his wide forehead; rubbed his chin thoughtfully; waved a casual greeting to a friend here, an acquaintance there. My stomach twisted. He looked like he'd already won every competition on offer. He looked like he owned the Igloo. And not just the Igloo. His other hand—the one that wasn't waving around like it was conducting an invisible orchestra—was resting possessively on Katie's denim-clad butt.

Gone were the days of the sloppy black T-shirt. Today, Katie looked way older than thirteen. She looked Jordan's age, at least. She was wearing real tight-fitting jeans—so tight I wondered how she'd managed to squeeze her feet through to get them on. Her legs went on forever. She had on this crinkly pink top that looked like she'd squashed it in a waffle-iron, held up by thin straps. She was looking up at Jordan, hanging on every word he uttered, laughing and preening and tossing her hair, and every now and again kind of nudging her hip against him. For a second I wondered whether Beattie had it right—whether *I* had it right.

Surely this couldn't be Katie? Her eyes looked bigger and wider—even her lips were a different color from how I remembered: a kind of glossy, paint-box pink.

"And over there is Santa Claus—and look! Rudolph the Red-Nosed Reindeer!"

"Huh?"

"Oh, so you are listening," said Beattie dryly. "You coulda fooled me. I'll let you in on a secret. I didn't win the Under Fourteen by skill alone, mind-boggling though my abilities are. No, the secret of my success is industrial espionage. You need to know your opposition. What they had for breakfast; their innermost hopes and deepest fears; the color of their underwear . . . the very texture of their toe-jam. And once you know them, you can beat 'em! And now, buster, you'd better head for that isolation room, along with the rest of the superjocks—and I hope you've got your designer gear under those cruddy old track pants, or I'll disown you."

"But—"

She gave me a none-too-gentle shove. "But nothing! Go on, Phil—they've called your class—or weren't you listening?" She rolled her eyes in exaggerated despair. "Honest—sometimes I think you need a keeper. See ya later. And hey—good luck. You're gonna need it, Spider-Man!"

A river of people was pouring into the gym, taking up their positions on the grandstand that had been erected in the center of the room. I pushed my way through them, clutching my bag, dizzy with sudden terror. It was about to start! What had I got myself into? I could pick out the other contestants easily now; I didn't even need Beattie. They were the only people making their way toward the entrance of the isolation room, against the flow of the tide—and they were all, without exception, about twice my height and built to match. They all moved with the fluid grace of top athletes, the confidence of professionals who'd done this countless times before.

Just before I ducked into the door of the isolation room, I felt a light touch on my arm. I gave a quick, hunted glance over my shoulder. What now? Was someone going to stop me from going in there? Was it so obvious I didn't belong? But it was Rob, in the faded old track top he always wore for coaching, his hair in its usual tangle, earring and crooked grin in place. Rob—same as ever. He gave me a quick wink; then turned and moved away through the crowd.

I watched his back disappear, feeling as if my last friend in the world were deserting me. And then—whether it was my heightened, panic-stricken senses or what, I don't know—I noticed—*really* noticed—the top he was wearing. The top he always wore, almost as familiar to me as my green T-shirt or striped pajamas. I'd always thought of it as mauve, but now I saw there was a kind of washed-out peppermint green in there as well . . . and fainter still, in an arc across the shoulders, the faded letters: HIGHLANDS.

A guy in a white coat was sitting at a table just inside the doorway, ticking off names on a list. I shuffled up, just behind a rangy-looking dark-skinned guy with a shaved head. I mumbled my name: "Phil—Phil McLeod." The official glanced up, somewhere above my head; then his gaze traveled down like a runaway elevator from the level the other guys' faces had been, to where mine was. He blinked; then gave me a slightly disapproving frown. "Good luck, sonny."

I'd never been in the isolation room before. There were two entrances: the one we'd come in through, and another one I guessed led directly out to the transition area and the climbing gym. Though the room was small, it was comfortably furnished with padded plastic chairs around the sides. A central table held a selection of climbing magazines, some a bit dog-eared. On the far wall was a high window, with the afternoon sun slanting through. It was slightly open, and I could hear the sound of distant traffic and a child's voice calling from far away. *I'm glad the real world's still out there somewhere*, I thought, and tossed my backpack onto a chair directly under it.

Another wall was obviously a warm-up area—fitted out like a proper bouldering wall, with cushioned matting underneath. Good. I'd need that later on. There was a soda machine over in the corner, next to a drinking fountain. Beside it was a door marked *Toilet*.

The old guy was levering himself to his feet and pottering over to us. "Right, gentlemen, listen carefully. I don't need to remind you this is an on-sight competition, unlike the junior events. You all know the routine—you've done this a hundred times before. Any questions, please ask. However, I'll run through the rules briefly . . . for the benefit of any newcomers." He shot me a dubious glance. Then he opened up his clipboard and began to read, in a rapid monotone. "On receiving an official instruction to leave the isolation zone to proceed to the transit zone, competitors shall not be accompanied by any person other than an authorized official . . ."

I swallowed. My mouth felt paper-dry, and my heart was beating a rapid, dizzying tattoo under my lucky shirt. There was a weird buzzing sound in my ears; I could hardly hear what the guy was saying. I shuffled closer. Some of the other climbers were carrying on whispered conversations. There was even some good-natured horseplay. They'd heard it all before.

"Each competitor shall be ready to leave the transit zone and enter the arena when instructed to do so. Any undue delay to do so may result in the immediate award of a yellow card; any further delay shall result in immediate disqualification . . ."

A deep voice spoke right behind me, very close, in an undertone; a warm gust of garlic breath wafted past my cheek. "Well, well, look who's here. Moo McLeod, come to play with the big boys."

I didn't turn. I'd had plenty of practice at ignoring Jordan Archer.

"Each competitor shall snaplink each carabiner or quick-draw in sequence. Each carabiner must be snaplinked before the lowest part of the competitor's body has moved above the lowest carabiner . . ."

GUMBY

"Hey, Gumby, *I'm talking to you!*"

I had a sudden image of Katie: Katie . . . and that hot, garlic breath. I knew I was going to throw up. I spun around and shot across the room, barged through the door marked *Toilet*, and held my head over the bowl, retching helplessly. As the door swung slowly closed behind me, I heard a sound I recognized all too well: Jordan Archer's mocking laughter.

THE SUNSET WALL

When I eventually emerged from the bathroom, the briefing was over and the straggle of climbers was disappearing through the swing door into the transition area for the preview. I hurried after them, the taste of vomit in my mouth, wishing I had time for a sip of water. I prayed I hadn't missed anything important.

I followed the other climbers through into the main auditorium. It looked like the first climb was going to be on what I'd always thought of as the "sunset wall" because of its geometric orange, yellow, and gray paintwork. It had harsh, angular topography and, like all the climbing walls in the Igloo, it varied in difficulty from easy to extremely severe, depending on which part you climbed. Though main features like the overhangs didn't change, the positioning, size, and shape of the holds made a huge difference to the route.

Standing on tiptoe, I craned my neck to see over the barricade of broad shoulders in front of me. I couldn't even see the beginning of the route! Then suddenly the tall figure directly blocking my view shifted and turned, and a lean, tanned face was peering down at me from a nest of dread-locks. A hard hand grabbed my shoulder, and I was propelled unceremoniously to the front of the group. It might have been my imagination, but I thought it gave a quick, encouraging squeeze before releasing me.

I took a deep breath and stared up at the climb. Like Rob had said, I'd previewed routes a thousand times before with-out even realizing I was doing it. Normally, it was as easy and instinctive as breathing. This time I was conscious of the intimidating cluster of climbers behind me—experienced, confident . . . and fiercely competitive. Their tense, focused silence unnerved me. What were they seeing that I wasn't? What should I be looking for? What might I be missing?

I glanced around. Over to my left, Jordan Archer was frowning with concentration and scribbling notes into a small black book, his lips set in a thin line. He gave a terse, satisfied nod, turned the page, and directed his gaze upward again. I realized what he was doing. He was noting the location of the clips, and where the key handholds were in relation to them. I should do that, too! I'd have sold my soul for some paper and a pen; but it was too late now.

Behind me, a voice spoke quietly: "Excuse me, I'd like to clarify a technical point. Flagging and smearing out of bounds—are they allowed?" The old guy who'd come with us from the isolation zone burbled some long-winded reply, but I didn't hear it. What the heck were they talking about? *Flagging and smearing?* They might as well have been speaking a foreign language. I didn't belong here!

"One minute," intoned the judge.

One minute? But wasn't the preview supposed to last six minutes? There was no way five whole minutes could have passed! "Excuse me," a high, quavering voice was asking. "Is that one minute *gone*, or one minute *to go?*" There was a snort of laughter from my left, and the judge's stony face cracked into a chilly smile. "One minute remaining," he said stuffily . . . and I'd barely had time to turn back to the wall and focus on the start of the climb before he was hustling us back the way we'd come.

The other climbers headed straight over to a notice board beside the door and stood there in a noisy cluster. There was a good deal of banter and joking around. Words I'd never heard before flew back and forth:

"Don't try to sandbag me . . ."

". . . needed another minute to finish my topo . . ."

". . . a move like that campus you pulled off in the Plains Open . . ."

They all seemed to know each other, like members of some secret society.

I flopped down on my chair under the window, dug out my water bottle, and took a sip. Washed it around my mouth and swallowed. The taste of vomit gurgled down my throat like dirty dishwater swirling down a drain. My stomach churned. I squeezed my eyes shut. *What's the matter with you?* I raged. *You're letting these guys psyche you out! If you don't get a grip on yourself, you might as well go home!* I needed to calm down. I needed to focus. Most of all, I needed to find out when I was climbing. The old guy would know. Then I needed to plan my warm-up, and review the route in my mind. Reluctantly, I opened my eyes.

Troy Gilmour was looking down at me. He had a long nose and bright green eyes, like a cat. Something told me they were eyes that could read a climb—read most things, probably—at a glance.

Right now, they were watching me intently. "Hey," he said quietly, "you okay? You look . . . kinda green around the gills."

I felt myself flush. "Yeah, I'm okay," I said. "Just—you know—reviewing the route . . . in my mind."

Troy Gilmour nodded. "Good plan. I won't interrupt. You're McLeod, aren't you? Phil McLeod?"

"Yeah," I admitted warily.

"Rob Gale mentioned you," he said with a grin, holding out his hand. "Says you're an ace climber—and from Rob, that really means something. I'm looking forward to seeing you in action. I'm Troy, by the way—Troy Gilmour."

"Hi," I croaked. I stood up, resisting the temptation to wipe my hand on the seat of my track pants. I knew it would feel like a dead fish—ice cold, and clammy with sweat. Troy Gilmour's grip was firm and dry, and radiated an almost electric energy.

"Hey, Phil—I don't want to interfere or anything, but . . . you might be thinking about warming up pretty soon."

"Warming up?"

"Yeah. You're up first, in . . ." he glanced at his watch, "less than five minutes."

My heart gave a lurch. *Five minutes?* "But—why didn't the guy say so? That judge guy, shouldn't he—"

"He did. During the briefing. The climbing order's on that list by the door. I thought you might not have realized." Troy smiled sympathetically. "Your first tournament's always tough. I remember mine. Wish I could forget it. What a train wreck! I'll tell you about it sometime. But right now, you need to warm up. I'll leave you to get on with it. And hey—good luck. Not that you'll need it." He gave me a nod and a smile, and turned away.

I stumbled to my feet and over to the deserted corner near the bouldering wall. Feeling as stiff and awkward as a marionette, I started my warm-up routine. But my eyes kept swiveling to the clock. The second hand twitched around, keeping time with my jerking heart. Infuriatingly, my brain was keeping count of the precious seconds as they slipped away: *fifty-four, fifty-five, fifty-six, fifty-seven, fifty-eight, fifty-nine, sixty, sixty-one . . .*

The old guy's voice rang out across the room, as if he were calling a condemned prisoner to the electric chair: "Contestant number one: Phil McLeod. Come with me. Your time is up."

"Step over the start line, please."

I took a wooden step forward. I couldn't feel my feet.

My hands were shaking. How was I going to climb? "You have forty seconds to commence your climb. Forty seconds from . . . *now*."

The auditorium was utterly silent. I stared stupidly at the orange wall in front of me. Looked up, up, up . . . the wall seemed to tilt and tip, as if it were about to fall on top of me.

"Twenty seconds."

I thought of all those people watching me. Beattie with her bright, dark eyes, spry as a little sparrow; Katie, beautiful and remote, waiting impatiently for me to finish so that Jordan could begin; Rob . . . and the look that'd be on his face when he realized he'd been wrong about me.

I thought of Dad.

Blindly, I reached for the nearest holds and began to climb. My movements were as jerky and uncoordinated as a wind-up toy. Almost immediately, I went wrong: where there should have been a hold, an easy hold, there was only emptiness. I downclimbed, fumbling for a foothold with toes I couldn't even feel; did an awkward, crab-like traverse, and then clambered clumsily upward again. I clipped the first bolt . . . the second . . . the third. My arms felt stiff and bloated. My fingers were slick as plastic, weak as a baby's. I needed to rest. I should have identified rest points on my preview; but I hadn't. The toughest part of the climb—the crux, an overhang it had taken me and Beattie two whole lessons to crack—was just ahead. And I wasn't even halfway.

Craning my head back, I squinted upward, looking for a place I could rest—I'd been climbing steadily since I started, and every muscle was on fire. I needed to take a break before I attacked the crux. If I didn't, I'd never make it. There'd been a good jug and two footholds a meter or two down the wall, but I'd pushed on past. Now, I wished I'd rested when I'd had the chance. Ahead, there was nothing. For a long moment I stalled in agonized indecision. What should I do? Downclimb again, wasting precious time and using up more energy, back to the rest I'd passed? Or push on? I hesitated, clinging to my holds, hands slippery with sweat. I needed to chalk up, but I didn't dare let go.

I took a shallow, shuddering breath and moved on up, gripping first one hold on the underside of the overhang . . . then another, with rubbery fingers. My body felt rigid and heavy; my hips wouldn't flex the right way. I felt my butt swing out into space . . . my hands slipped off the holds as if they were made of ice. I dropped from the wall like an over-ripe plum, and fell for what seemed like forever before the rope finally pulled me up with a sickening jerk and I swung there helplessly.

I'd failed. Failed Beattie, failed Rob . . . and most important of all, failed myself.

COUNTBACK

Head bowed, sick at heart, I headed for the roped-off section of the grandstand reserved for competitors after their climb. There'd been a scattered smattering of sympathetic applause when I touched down, but it was the drawn-out "aaaaahh-hhh" when I'd fallen that still rang in my ears. The others would have heard it, too, behind the closed doors of the isolation room. They'd know I was out of the competition—and most of them wouldn't be one bit surprised. I sat down, put my head in my hands, and closed my eyes. It was over before it had even begun.

Then I felt a compact little form hunker down next to me, giving me a shove to make more room. From farther away, a male voice spoke reprovingly: "You can't sit there. That section's for competitors only."

"Oh yes, I can," retorted Beattie. "I'm his . . . *sports psychologist*. So butt out."

My lips twitched in spite of myself. I opened my eyes. There was Beattie's face, centimeters from mine, glaring at me. Beyond her I could see a guy in a white coat, mouth open, stunned. Beattie was enough to stun anyone. It wouldn't last, though; and once he'd recovered, he'd move in for the kill.

Beattie couldn't care less. "What the heck happened to you?" she hissed loudly. "You climbed like a constipated hippopotamus! Have you had a brain transplant or something?"

The official blinked and backed off a step or two.

"I dunno what went wrong." I looked down again to avoid meeting her eyes. "I guess I don't have what it takes."

Beattie said a very rude word. Up at the wall the next competitor had started his climb, moving from hold to hold with fluid grace.

"Beattie . . ." I didn't want to know the answer, but I couldn't help asking. "What's a gumby?"

"It's what I thought you were that first day: a beginner, a rookie, green as grass and wet behind the ears. Something you've never been, Spider-Man. Though the way you climbed just now . . . *well* . . ."

"Beattie—enough." There on my other side was Rob. The one person I'd most dreaded seeing. All his hard work—for nothing. I braced myself for the harsh words I knew I deserved—for blame, contempt, anger, and bitter disappointment.

"I'm sorry," I croaked.

"*Sorry?* What for?"

"For messing up. For letting you down."

"That's garbage. But this isn't the place to discuss it. Come with me." Together, we made our way through the hushed stadium to the door, and out into the corridor. The poster was still there, faded and dog-eared. Like me, it had done its run.

"Listen, Phil," Rob said sternly, "you need to lighten up. I'll admit that wasn't your best climb. But it was your first competitive climb—and it wasn't as bad as most, believe me. Look on the bright side. It's over, behind you forever. Things can only get better." Hesitantly, hardly daring to hope he meant it, I looked up and met his eyes. They smiled down at me, warm with understanding and encouragement.

A burst of applause came from the stadium. "Even if that's true," I said miserably, "it doesn't change the fact that I've blown it. After that pathetic climb, there's no way I'll make it to the next round."

To my astonishment, Rob threw back his head and laughed. "So that's what's bothering you! Remember what I told you, Phil? Golden rule number one: pay attention at the briefing. Didn't they tell you about the practice round—to warm up, and determine the official competition climbing order? I bet your head was in the clouds, same as always, and you didn't listen. Well, listen now: no matter what, that climb won't count toward your score. It'll probably mean you end up climbing first in the initial round . . . but in many ways, that's an advantage. Gives you less time to sweat—and a great chance to check out the competition.

I gaped at him. "You . . . you mean . . . *I get a second chance?*"

He grinned down at me. "That's exactly what I mean.

And I'll tell you something, Phil. A second chance is a gift we're not often given in life. When you're offered one, grab it with both hands—especially if it's a chance at something you've realized is important. Make the most of it—and don't be afraid to take a few risks."

I stood at the bottom of the midnight blue wall, roped up and ready to go. My rack of quickdraws hung from my harness, heavy and reassuring. The image of the route was fresh and clear as a map in my mind, learned in the preview. My muscles felt loose, elastic, ready to roll. My breathing was deep and even.

"Step over the start line."

I took a long, smooth stride forward. Almost of their own accord, my hands reached confidently for the first holds. Though I'd never done this route before—never seen it till fifteen minutes ago—they felt like old friends, as big and solid as pot handles. From somewhere far away, as if in another world, I heard a child's voice: "Isn't that the first boy, Mum—the one who messed up?"

Another voice: "Shhhh!"

No, I answered her in my mind. *It's not. It's a different person altogether.*

Then I left all conscious thought behind me, and began to climb.

Only two people reached the top on that first round. Troy Gilmour was one, and I was the other.

COUNTBACK

Watching the others fall off the wall one by one—some, like Jordan, from close to the top, but one or two just over halfway—I realized what an elite group I was competing in. Technically, every one of them was my superior. Rob was right—they had the advantage over me in almost every way. But I was light, and skinny, and strong. I had good timing, and—if Rob was right—some God-given X-factor that defied definition. Even that wouldn't be enough to get me through; I knew that now.

But there was one other thing I had which they didn't. I was the underdog. And that meant that, unlike them, I had nothing to lose.

I fell off the second climb—Stairway to Heaven, a crippling series of buttressed overhangs—two clips from the top. I'd tried a dyno to get past a tricky section where the holds had been positioned far apart, a challenge to climbers way taller than me. The dyno—a dynamic jump up and to the right—was supposed to transfer me to a simpler sequence of holds. From there, topping out would be a breeze. It was the major crux area of my climb. Like Rob said, it was a risk. A calculated risk; and one that didn't work.

Swinging from the rope, I heard the wave of applause from the crowd far below and felt a surge of triumph. I'd done my best. If I made it through to the final, it would be way more than I—or anyone else—had ever expected. And if I didn't . . . well, there was always next time.

An expectant hush fell over the crowd. The mike gave a high-pitched electronic whine; then a series of furry huffs as the judge blew into it. He cleared his throat. "Ladies and gentlemen, boys and girls, I am pleased to announce our four finalists. As your names are read out, please make your way to the isolation room to await the final round. The finalists are . . ." he extracted a piece of paper from his pocket, unfolded it, and peered at it shortsightedly.

"Hope he can read them," whispered Beattie.

I dug her in the ribs. "Shhhh. Listen."

"Scott Harris." A tough-looking guy with a buzz cut and a pierced eyebrow vaulted down from the grandstand. I caught a glimpse of a tattoo on one shoulder, half hidden by his vest. Like all the other climbers, he was lean, tanned, and athletic. He lifted one hand casually to acknowledge the applause, and sauntered toward the door.

"Troy Gilmour." The cheers and clapping redoubled. Troy slid off his perch near the top of the grandstand and dropped lightly to the ground. With the glimmer of a smile in the general direction of the crowd, he walked over to join Scott Harris. They were waiting to hear who they'd be up against—and who could blame them?

"Jordan Archer." An excited squeal went up from somewhere in the crowd—a squeal I recognized. Then Jordan was on his feet, shaking hands with his coach and smirking to the left and right as he swaggered across to join his friends.

Unbelievably, the grim face of the judge relaxed into an actual smile. "And last but by no means least: our youngest competitor, in his debut tournament—Phil McLeod!"

The stadium erupted. I felt my face turn red. Beattie clapped me on the back so hard I nearly fell off my seat. Clumsily, I scrambled down to ground level and stumbled across the floor, tripping over my shoelace along the way. I didn't dare look at the crowd, in case someone saw the disbelief in my eyes. *I'd made it to the final!* Whatever happened now was a bonus. A gift, like the second chance I'd already been given.

This time, I'd be the last to climb. Now I understood why Rob said it was an advantage to go first. Waiting in the isolation room was torture. I took regular, small sips of water to keep hydrated. I paid a visit to my old friend the toilet, although I didn't really need to—just to be sure. I nibbled on one of Mum's special oat crunchies, even though it seemed dry and tasteless.

I closed my eyes and played through the climb ahead in my mind. I wondered if everyone could remember every hold, every bolt, every bump and crack and mottle in the wall, the way I seemed able to do. Troy could, I felt sure. But I bet Jordan couldn't—otherwise, why would he need his little black book? I grinned to myself, suddenly feeling much more cheerful.

I watched the other climbers do gentle warm-ups, and learned from it. After three climbs, we were already pretty pumped. More important now was to conserve our energy.

Scott Harris's name was called, and he disappeared through the doors into the transition area. I stood near the doorway and did a few gentle stretches. If I concentrated hard, I could just make out the tiny metallic clicks of his cara- biners as he made his way slowly up the wall. If I closed my eyes, I could picture exactly which point he'd reached . . . *Stop it. You're psyching yourself out again.*

I went back to my bag and checked my gear one last time. Then I sat down on my chair under the window, closed my eyes, concentrated on relaxing and breathing deeply . . . and waited.

Finally, I was alone in the room . . . and then, at last, it was my turn.

The tension in the stadium crackled like blue static as I walked slowly to the foot of the wall. *Ten minutes maxi- mum, and it will all be over. One way . . . or another.*

And then I was climbing again, one move following the next like notes of music, like sparkling water flowing along a riverbed. Time . . . the stadium . . . the crowd . . . the other competitors . . . everything ceased to exist, except me and the wall.

The last few holds were like clambering from a trance back into the real world. It was only as I reached for the final handhold that the enormity of it finally hit me. I'd made it! I was at the top—topping out in the final! A tidal wave of applause roared up to meet me. If I'd unclipped and let go I could have surfed down on it, bobbing on the waves of sound, as light and buoyant as a cork.

Then I was on the ground, Beattie pushing her way past the officials and throwing her arms around me; Rob grinning across at me over a sea of heads; Troy clapping me on the shoulder; and Jordan turning away, his face like thunder.

The loudspeaker was crackling and burping, battling to make itself heard over the hubbub of the crowd. "Ladies and gentlemen! Ladies and gentlemen, could I have your attention, please! Could we have silence! Silence, now—or I shall be obliged to clear the stadium! We have an unprecedented situation. Two climbers have topped out in the final round. The accepted procedure is for a countback, with the scores of the tied competitors in the previous two rounds totaled and the climber with the highest score winning the competition."

A buzz broke out again. "In the first round, Phil McLeod topped out, gaining maximum points. In the second round, the reverse situation occurred. And in the third round, both competitors are equal. But on the routes where the two climbers fell, both scored identical points. This means the two climbers are exactly equal. The judges have called for the climbers to face each other in one last contest. There will be a superfinal between our joint leaders: Phil McLeod . . . and Jordan Archer!"

MOO

The isolation zone was a welcome oasis of silence after the commotion of the main stadium. A half-hour break had been announced to allow the route setter to set a climb hard enough to separate the two finalists. Me . . . and Jordan.

"You can do it, Phil," Beattie had hissed in my ear, hopping alongside as the white-coated official led us away to the door. "You don't have to top out—*no one* tops out in a superfinal! You just have to go one hold higher—one measly hold! And you can do it, Spider-Man!"

From Rob, there'd just been a crooked smile, a pat on the shoulder, and a simple "Great climb, kid. Remember—no pressure, huh? When the time comes, go out there and have fun. And until then . . . relax."

That was what I was doing now. I was sprawled in my chair, hands locked behind my head, legs stretched out in front of me. I'd taken off my climbing shoes, and my toes were wiggling luxuriously. Through half-closed eyes, I was watching Jordan. He'd produced a small, square mirror from his bag, and was inspecting what I assumed must be an invisible zit on one side of his chin. Then he fished out a comb, and started rearranging his hair.

I grinned to myself. I'd be prepared to bet gazing at his own reflection was Jordan's favorite way of relaxing—and his major source of inspiration.

The official was back at his desk by the door, a climbing magazine open in front of him. His head was gradually sagging lower and lower; then it would give a little nod and a sudden jerk as he jolted awake again. It had been a long day.

I sipped some water and glanced at the clock. Five-thirty. Fifteen minutes to go. I was climbing first. And one thing was for sure: this time I'd be ready.

A cold, damp breeze was blowing down my neck from the open window. Glancing up, I saw it was practically dark outside. A strange, uncomfortable feeling tingled gently under my ribcage. Something was wrong. *Nerves. Just nerves.*

I stood and turned to close the window. *Almost dark . . . five-thirty . . .* And that's when I heard it. A faint, jingling tune from far away, growing steadily closer. A tune as familiar to me as the musical mobile above my baby sister's cot . . . Then, faint but unmistakable, another sound. Moo. *Moooo.*

The realization hit me like a bucket of ice water. The tingling morphed into a knife blade, slicing into my gut. *Five-thirty. The milk run. Dad.*

On Fridays we started from the bottom of the hill, so we could drop Nick at the Igloo for his indoor cricket. Dad would be dropping him off now; then he'd be heading away, on his own, to start the run. He'd be wondering where the hell I was. He'd be livid.

Jordan's voice cut into my jumble of thoughts. "Well, would you listen to that? Little Moo McLeod's daddy's coming to watch him climb! And he's brought one of the cows with him . . ."

But I'd stopped listening. Dad wasn't coming to watch me climb. He didn't even know I was here.

A voice echoed in my mind. Rob's voice, as clear as if he were standing next to me: *A second chance is a gift we're not often given in life. When you're offered one, grab it with both hands—especially if it's a chance at something you've realized is important. Make the most of it—and don't be afraid to take a few risks.*

Then I was heading for the door at a run—but not the door to the transition area: the door to the corridor, where the old official was dozing. I caught a flash of Jordan's shocked face as I pushed past him, knocking him flying. As I yanked the door open, the official jerked wide awake: "*Hey!* You can't . . ."

I could.

I raced down the corridor, dodging to avoid the steady flow of people heading back from the refreshment kiosk. One little kid had fallen over; he was lying there yelling his head off in a snowdrift of popcorn. Without breaking stride, I leapt clean over him, and ran on.

I raced through the main auditorium, nearly colliding with Nick at the front entrance. His face broke into a grin.

"Thought you'd be here! You're gonna *really* catch it! Dad—"

I ducked past him, and ran on. Out into the dark parking lot, still crammed with cars. I stared wildly around. No sign of the milk truck. Then—*yes!* There it was! Over at the gate, waiting for a gap in the traffic, its brake lights reflecting red as blood on the slick, wet tar. I sprinted through the drizzle, the tarmac hurting my feet, shouting hoarsely: "Dad! *Dad!*"

Then the truck was pulling away, turning into the traffic. Desperately, hopping from foot to foot, I waited for a break in the stream of cars, then raced across the road. A truck honked and the driver wound down his window and yelled something, but I didn't care. I was focused on the back view of the milk truck. It was heading away from me toward the traffic light, way faster than I could run. I lost sight of it . . . but still, I raced on.

The traffic light! The light was red! Dad would have to stop! Sobbing, my breath burning like fire in my lungs, I pounded on down the street, past the long line of cars waiting for the light to change.

Now I could see the truck up ahead again, at the front of the line. Dad's blinker was flicking. . . . He'd be turning into the long street leading to Ballinger Park. And once he made that turn, I'd have lost him.

The light changed to green. "*No!* Dad! *Dad . . .*"

But it was too late. I was almost close enough to touch the back of the truck when the engine roared and it began to move, turning into Ballinger Street and accelerating away.

I pelted around the corner after it, my bare feet raw on the rough surface, my arms waving frantically. *"Dad! Dad!"*

Then my ankle gave way under me, twisting so I almost fell. Agony shot through my foot like a blade, and I hobbled to a stop. Up ahead, the milk truck was disappearing into the night. Dumbly, shoulders slumped, I watched as it drew farther and farther away. My breath was coming in huge, agonizing gasps; my face was wet with rain and sweat and tears.

And then the brake lights flashed on, red in the darkness. The truck slowed and pulled over to the side of the road, out of the traffic. The backup lights shone out golden in the dusk as Dad's milk truck started reversing toward me, making its familiar *beep—beep—beep*.

I limped toward it as fast as I could. Wrenched open the passenger door. Dad glowered at me, face black as a storm cloud. "I saw you in the rear-view mirror. *Where have you been?* Just what the *hell* . . ."

His gaze rasped over me like sandpaper. He took in my soaking hair and tear-stained face; my lucky green T-shirt and skuzzy shorts; and my skinny goose bumped legs. His face began to change. "Son—are you all right?"

I slid into the truck beside him, my eyes locked on his face. I reached out one small, frozen hand, and put it tentatively on the big, warm one gripping the steering wheel. *Please*, I prayed, *let this work—for both of us.*

"Dad. You need to come with me. Please. Don't ask why. Just . . . just trust me. Come quickly. *Please!*"

Dad shook his head slowly from side to side in grim disbelief. Shrugged his broad shoulders. Then he put the truck in gear and followed my directions back to the Igloo.

With Dad limping behind me in bamboozled silence, I hustled my way back through the indoor sports arena and down the passage to the Climbing Center. At the isolation room door, I stopped. "Dad—see there, up ahead? The stadium? Go in and sit down. You have to watch—please! But I can't come in with you. I'm not allowed to see the wall. What's the time? I have to—"

The isolation room door flew open, and the old official popped out like an irate jack-in-the-box. "There you are!" he snapped. A hand shot out and gripped my arm like a vice, and I was yanked into the room.

"*Please*, Dad!" I wailed desperately.

Then the door slammed between us, and the wrath of the Climbing Federation broke over my head.

JORDAN'S CHOICE

Five stony-faced officials in white coats stood around me in a semi-circle, like avenging angels. One—the oldest and most senior, who'd announced himself as the chief judge—held a red book in his hand.

"The rule book states clearly: *It is the responsibility of all contestants to familiarize themselves with competition regulations prior to the event.* Furthermore, here we have, under point number 8.1.1, and I quote: *No contestant may leave the isolation zone for any reason whatever other than to proceed with a designated official to the transition zone.* And here, point 8.1.3: *No contestant may under any circumstances whatever observe the route, or attempt to observe the route, from outside the permitted observation zone.* The rule book is quite explicit."

"But—"

"Silence, young man! The rule book continues, under point number 8.1.6: *Infringement of any of the above regulations shall result in the issuing of a Red Card and the immediate disqualification of the competitor from the competition, and subsequent referral to the disciplinary commission."*

"I—"

"Young man, it seems you still don't appreciate the enormity of your offense." He frowned severely down at me. "Do you understand—"

There was a token thump on the door, and it flew open. Every head in the room swiveled to see who had come barging in. "What now?" The chief judge sighed. "This is all *highly* irregular . . ."

Nick stood in the doorway. I gaped at him. So did the officials; so did Jordan, from his seat in the corner.

"And who might *you* be?"

Nick's cheeks were flushed and his eyes flashed. I'd felt like a toddler hemmed in by the intimidating row of officials; but Nick was every bit as big as them. He stared them right in the face, eyeball to eyeball.

"Hey—I heard you're going to chuck Pip out of the competition 'cause he went to get Dad!" His foghorn voice sounded loud in the confined space of the isolation room. It also sounded angry. "Is that right?"

The chief judge took a small step backward. I would've, too, with Nick's face so close to mine, and that look on his face. "I—who is Pip? And who, pray, are you?"

"I'm Nick McLeod, his brother. *Is* it true?"

"Ah . . . well . . . the situation is extremely grave . . ."

"Listen. You guys are blowing this thing out of proportion.

It's spread through the whole building like wildfire—that's how I got to hear about it. But one thing's for sure: Pip only went one place. And that was straight outside and back again. He never went near the climbing stadium. He only went out to fetch Dad, so he could watch him climb. If you throw him out of the final just for that—well, it sucks. And so do you."

The chief judge blinked. There was an uncomfortable pause. In the silence, my friend the dozing official put his hand up to his mouth and gave a little choking cough. Then, unexpectedly, he spoke:

"There is a certain amount of merit in what this young fellow has to say. The point at issue is the unauthorized gathering of information relating to the superfinal route. It appears that such an infringement has not, in fact, taken place."

"Damn right," agreed Nick forcefully.

The chief judge sighed again. He frowned down at me. "Well, young man? Did you access the climbing stadium during your absence? Did you obtain any information relating to the route, of any nature, from any source whatever?"

I shook my head. A tiny, tentative flicker of hope flared inside me. Maybe—just maybe—I'd be allowed to climb after all.

The chief judge turned to Jordan, uncharacteristically silent in the corner. "And what about you, Mr. Archer? You would be well within your rights to lodge an official protest against Mr. McLeod. If you do, it would probably give you victory by default. Please make your intention clear—do you wish to lodge a complaint, or are you willing to proceed with the superfinal?"

Everyone looked at Jordan, sitting there with his hair artfully tousled and an expression of uncertainty on his face. Watching the indecision in his eyes, I knew exactly what he was thinking. *I can lodge the objection and win this right now, without even having to climb again. But then again— my moment of glory. My hairdo. My girlfriend, waiting in the stands to see me triumph. The chance to show this little runt who's top dog.*

He looked sharply across at me—a concentrated, calculating look. Just how much of a threat did I pose to him, really?

Not much, was the answer. Though I'd got my breath back from my frantic dash through the darkness, Jordan knew where I'd gone, and how long I'd been away. He could see how wet I was, and how tired. Though I hadn't walked more than a step or two since I'd come into the room, his eyes kept sliding down to my left ankle, and I was sure he'd noticed me favoring it.

While he'd been resting up, nibbling on carbohydrates and maybe doing a few gentle stretches, I'd been chasing around the city after my dad, getting freezing cold, using up all my energy, reducing my feet to mincemeat . . . and doing who knew what to my ankle.

I watched Jordan's mouth twitch into an almost invisible smile. For something you could barely see, it managed to

radiate an amazing amount of satisfaction. He rose grace-
fully to his feet, his tall, broad-shouldered form in its
designer gear making me feel like a ragged street urchin.

"Okay," he said. "We climb. Phil's just a gumby, after all.
He didn't know any better. But I'm a sportsman, first and
last. Let's do it."

I was shivering as I struggled into the borrowed shorts and
climbing vest the old official had brought me. As unobtrusively as I could, I probed my left ankle, gently rotating my
foot. Something was wrong, that was for sure. How bad it
was, only time would tell.

I pulled on my sweatshirt and dug in my bag for an
energy bar. I wasn't hungry, but I had to eat to warm up and
replace some of that lost energy. Hardest of all, I had to
somehow get my mental balance back.

But images and questions were flooding my mind. Nick—
who'd have thought it? And the grouchy old official!
Unexpected allies, both of them—but effective. I wondered
where Rob was, and what he was making of all this. And
Beattie. I wondered about the climb. Which one? How hard
would it be? Could I climb, with my ankle the way it was?

Above all, I thought about Dad. I could see his face in my
mind . . . but no matter how hard I tried, I couldn't read his
expression. Would he be mad? He'd know I'd fibbed about the
photography club. Lying was a cardinal sin in our house.

Most important: would he stay to watch me climb? Dad's

milk run was carved in stone. To his customers, it didn't matter a tinker's fart—as Nick was fond of saying—whether the milk arrived at six o'clock or twenty past. But to Dad, it was a matter of life and death. Would he still be there, sitting in his MooZical Milk windbreaker with the rest of the spectators? Somehow, I couldn't see it.

"Gentlemen: will you please accompany me into the stadium for the preview."

Without looking at each other, Jordan and I followed the old guy into the auditorium. There was a tense, expectant silence; then someone started to clap, and a scattered current of applause swept uncertainly across the grandstand, like a ragged wave. Jordan acknowledged it with a casual hand. I followed slowly in his wake, trying to disguise my limp. My eyes were scanning the crowd, searching for Dad's face. My heart sank. He wasn't there. He'd gone.

And then I saw him—right on the bottom row, near the end. His face was as expressionless as ever, his arms folded across his chest. There next to him, chirping away like a demented cockatoo, was Beattie. On his other side, Nick. He was supposed to be umpiring the cricket! But he wasn't. He was there, watching me. Seemed to me no one was where they were supposed to be that night. Then again, maybe they were.

That was the last thought I had time for before we stopped at the foot of the superfinal route, and the judge intoned: "You have six minutes, gentlemen. Six minutes . . . from . . . *now*."

The Morning After.

Rob had told me once that the climb was given this name because it had so many hangovers. Of all the walls in the Igloo, it was way the most challenging, an imitation granite face on the outer wall. Because of the shape of the building, it followed an inward curve, with the top a good couple of meters in from the bottom; but it wasn't a gradual curve. Shelves, buttresses, cracks, and crevices imitated a natural cliff face. Even the holds were colored to match the wall, making them hard to identify—and harder still to evaluate with any accuracy.

Climbing The Morning After was the closest you'd ever get indoors to climbing a real cliff. Beattie and I had clambered around on the lower levels for fun; Rob had set us a couple of his special challenges higher up—to take us down a peg or two, I suspected. But I'd never actually climbed it seriously—and never seen anyone climb it right to the top.

All this spun through my mind as my eyes worked their way gradually up the rock face, catching on protrusions here, snagging on minute holds there. Like an invisible zigzag, the route revealed itself to me. Not the most direct route. Not this time. The route I'd need to take with my damaged ankle—a route that relied more heavily on my right foot than my left. A nightmare climb . . . but possible. Maybe. Except for one section way up near the top . . . a crux to end all cruxes . . . The timer pinged, and the preview was over.

Five minutes later, roped up, rack at my waist, hands

chalked and ready to go, I was following the official's white-clad back out to the stadium again.

"Step over the line." I stepped forward. "You have forty seconds in which to commence your climb."

A part of my mind expected to hear Dad's voice cracking through the silence like a bullwhip: "Go, Son, go! Faster, faster! Higher, *higher*!" My head twitched around in reflex, as if I'd really heard him yell out. My eyes locked on him, there in the corner of the grandstand. Beattie was clutching his arm in an agony of nerves, her face ashen and intent.

Dad's mouth under his bristly mustache was shut tight as a steel trap. His eyes were fixed on me, deadpan. There was nothing in his face to show that I was his son . . . nothing to show he knew who I was, or cared. For a second, our eyes met. Then the crow's-feet around Dad's eyes deepened, and one eye flickered shut in an almost invisible wink.

And then it wasn't about me and Dad anymore. It wasn't even about me and Jordan.

It was about me and the wall. I turned back, took a deep breath, and began to climb.

SUPERFINAL

The first part would have been easy, if it hadn't been for my ankle. As soon as I put serious pressure on it, a flare of pain shot up my leg into my groin. The world dimmed and swayed as a wave of nauseating faintness swept through me. I hung desperately onto my solid handholds; rested my weight on my good leg. Took shallow, careful breaths. Had a brief, unscheduled rest. Took stock.

The question isn't whether you can deal with the pain, because you don't have a choice, I told myself fiercely. *The only question is whether the leg will hold up for the next few minutes . . . even if it feels like forever.*

Mentally, I stashed the pain behind me, somewhere in the region of my chalk bag. I'd take it along for the ride; I had no choice. But I'd put it where it wouldn't be too much in the way.

I took a deep, steadying breath and looked up at the cliff rearing above me. I saw myself at the top, raising one clenched fist above my head. I held the image in my mind, clear as a memory, vivid as a photograph. Then I moved my hand to the next hold, flexed my good leg, and moved smoothly on up the wall.

At the midpoint, I clipped the bolt and stopped for another rest. So far, so good, but there was a tough section just ahead—a section I'd normally have skipped with a dyno. This time I'd just have to power through it. The wall was textured, rough like real rock; I found myself using bumps I could barely see, almost wriggling up the rock like a snake. Finally, I could see the next bolt up ahead. But to reach it, I'd have to use my left leg. I felt gingerly for the ledge I knew was there; found it, gritted my teeth, and levered myself powerfully upward on my bad leg. Pain seared through me like a red-hot skewer, fizzing in my brain and draining my strength away. A film of greasy sweat sprang out all over me. My right hand slipped from its hold. The stadium swam. I was going . . . going . . . *No! Not now!*

Desperately, instinctively, I rammed my left hand into a vertical crack in the rock face, clenching my fist so it wedged solid in the narrow opening. The fist jam locked me onto the wall like a bolt. I swung to the left, carried by the momentum of my lunge; my right foot found the ledge. I dangled precariously, one foot firm, one hand firm, until gradually, with agonizing slowness, the faintness faded.

I chalked up my right hand; then switched, and chalked the left. Automatically, my eyes looked ahead. What now? I didn't want to downclimb. Hang on—there was a useful-looking sequence over to the right. A good hold—no, a *great* hold—then a simple progression up to that elusive bolt. Just one problem: to get to the hold, I'd have to risk a jump—a leap of faith, propelled by my one good foot. If I locked onto the hold—if my fingers held—I'd be away and laughing. If not . . .

I double-checked. Was there an alternative to that jump? Was there a higher foothold I could reach? There wasn't. Nothing else to do, then. Judging the distance carefully, focusing on the target hold, I readied myself. Sank as low as I could on my foothold, to maximize the thrust. Positioned my hands, gripping better now with the fresh chalk, ready to steer me through the move.

Speed . . . accuracy . . . contact.

One . . . two . . . *three!*

I launched myself into nothingness. It was as if time stretched into slow motion, freeze-frame following freeze-frame as I arced through the air. And then my hand was locking onto the hold, my foot was edged into a narrow diagonal crack, and I was swarming on up to the bolt on a wave of adrenaline.

That adrenaline rush carried me over the next two cruxes as if they weren't there. Even with my ankle, I knew I was climbing better than I ever had before. My body felt lean and as supple as a monkey's. I couldn't put much weight on my bad leg; but in some ways, one foot was working better than two ever had. With one foot and two hands on, I could use my other foot like a pendulum—like a monkey's tail—to swing me from one dynamic combination to the next. With the speed came a wonderful, wild, rhythmic momentum, propelling me up the route as if it were a jungle gym.

And then I was there—at that final, crucial crux. I chalked up, and took five to plan my attack. This was the one section where I didn't have a solution, but that didn't bother me—not the way I was climbing. Eyes narrowed, I scanned the holds ahead. *Yeah!* That was it! A solid, slightly indented, elongated hold up and away to my left. I wouldn't be able to stretch to it; but a strong shove off with my good right foot, helped along by a pendulum swing of my left, and I'd be there. Grab it; swing up to the next; a good cup-shaped foothold to consolidate the move . . . and then plain sailing to the top. *The top!*

This dyno was nothing compared to the one I'd cracked before. I chalked up, judged my distance. Leapt.

Perfect! My fingers made contact with the rough surface of the hold, curling snugly into the indent . . . and then the impossible happened. The hold swiveled and spun under my hand. The surface that had been horizontal—a perfect hold—tilted nightmarishly around to the vertical; my fingers slid helplessly away . . . and I was falling into space.

That second froze into eternity. I was falling, spinning, my mind one huge, silent cry of denial. *Noooooooooooooooo!*

My left hand shot out instinctively and latched onto the cup-like foothold I'd seen just below, nearly wrenching my shoulder from its socket. I dangled helplessly, all my energy focused on that one grip. Hang on—*hang on!*

My body gave a twist and a lunge, and my other hand

was wedged in a crack. Two hands solid. My feet scrabbled and kicked against the rock . . . found a toehold. My heart was hammering hard enough to knock me right off the rock . . . but my move—disastrous though it had almost been—had taken me onto the line I'd been heading for— even without that treacherous hold, I was home free.

Moments later, unbelievably, I was reaching for the second-to-last hold; then the last . . . and I was there, topping out on The Morning After, with the world going wild way, way below.

My feet touched down and my legs turned to jelly. My ankle finally gave out on me, dumping me unceremoniously on the floor, my face one ginormous grin. Over by the grandstand, there was pandemonium. People were on their feet, clapping and cheering; I caught a glimpse of Beattie capering around in a crazy dance and Rob pushing through the crush of bodies toward me, his face a kaleidoscope of emotions.

Cautiously I levered myself up. My ankle felt weird—hot and swollen with the skin stretched tight, like a sausage frying in a pan. But it was numb, for now at least.

Over at the judges' table, Jordan's coach was yelling something, his voice lost in the general hubbub. I half-hopped, half-hobbled closer. He was leaning over the table, both hands flat on its surface, his face millimeters from the chief judge. "He fell!" he was yelling. "McLeod fell and continued the climb! I wish to lodge an official protest! *Two* protests! That kid should never have been allowed to climb! He left the isolation zone for ten minutes—it's common knowledge! He could have gone anywhere—spoken to anyone! He could never have done that climb without prior knowledge of the route. He should never have been allowed in this age group! He—"

Another judge was on his feet now, arguing with the coach. He had some kind of clipboard in his hand and was pointing to it, shoving it under the coach's nose, trying to get his attention. A rhythmic chant had started up over at the grandstand: "*Phil McLeod! Phil McLeod! Phil McLeod!*" Then Rob was shouldering his way over to the mob gathered around the judges' table. For a second I heard his voice clearly through the babble, not raised like all the rest, but quiet, measured, reasonable: ". . . technical incident . . . the hold that spun . . ."

Then I turned my back on it all, and awkwardly hopped over to Dad. He was on his feet with the rest of the spectators, looking lost and helpless, and hopelessly out of place. I grabbed his hand. "C'mon, Dad—let's go."

"Go? But don't you want to—"

"Nah. I've done enough." And I had. I'd done what I set out to—and more.

"Come on, Dad. We're late. We've got a milk run to do."

THE FIFTH MANDARIN

Start . . . stop . . . start . . . stop. The musical jingle of the milk truck carried us through the darkness from one island of light to the next. Moo. *Moooo!*

In spite of my protests Dad insisted on helping me, leaving the truck patiently idling as he took one side of the road, me the other. "You shouldn't be walking on that leg at all," he said when I objected.

A few streets later, as we limped back together toward the truck, he shot me a sidelong glance from under his bushy eyebrows, glinting with rueful humor. "Fine pair we make, huh, Son?"

I grinned back.

We sure did: a fine pair.

At last, we reached the end of the run; I stashed the last heavy plastic holder behind the last mailbox, hopped along to the passenger door, and slid inside. Dad looked over at me, his familiar scowl in place, his eyes full of concern. "We'll get your mother to wrap that ankle the minute we get home. Then it's rest, ice, compression, elevation—and no more heroics." Dad learned all that stuff about injury treatment from his firefighting days. "You know you were crazy to pull that stunt back there, don't you?"

I tried to look repentant, but the grin didn't help—and it wouldn't go away. "Sure, Dad."

Dad's mustache bristled, and he huffed out through his nose. Shook his head slowly. Seemed there was plenty he wanted to say. Not much of it good, I reckoned. But he put the truck in gear in silence, and we glided away down the hill toward home.

And then suddenly, like a dam bursting, my words came—a flood of telling, after all those long weeks of silence.

"... all started completely by accident, as if it was somehow *meant* ... went to the Igloo before it opened ... snuck in ... climbed right to the top ... in real bad trouble ... Rob said I should come back again ... you ... Mum ... soccer ... something I'm good at—*truly* good at ... not really a lie—I did *think* about doing photography, honest ... really, really cool—*supercool* ... Beatrix, like Beatrix Potter, even crazier than me ... didn't want to enter ... *meant* to be on time ... heard the truck ... suddenly *knew* ... *being and knowing* ... hard to explain, I guess ..."

The words ran down pretty much the same time as the truck turned into our driveway. The lights of home shone out in the darkness. Dad turned off the engine. We sat there together for a long moment. "Dad—are we friends again?"

He turned to me. The whaley smile shone from his eyes,

warm as sunshine. "What do you think? Sure, we're friends again."

But there was stuff that still needed to be said.

"Dad—what happened that day. I—I'm sorry . . . for some of it, anyhow. The way it came out. I didn't mean it."

Dad looked at me, the ghost of the smile still in his eyes. "I think you did. But sometimes things have to be said. Maybe it should have been said sooner. It doesn't do to keep things bottled up." He took out his handkerchief and blew his nose, the way he does when he's playing for time. Then he polished his mustache, the way he does. "I'm no good with words—your mother knows that. Feelings, emotions— it's her kind of thing. Me, I just fumble my way through. But I had no idea how you felt . . . about that . . . that soccer thing. No idea at all. Next time 'round, if something's bothering you, trust me with it—just a little bit sooner. Okay?"

"Okay, Dad." My voice was the merest whisper in the dark.

"And Son . . ."

"Yes, Dad?"

"I'm not much good at saying this kind of thing . . . not enough practice, I guess." We waited. "But—I'm proud of you. Was especially proud of you, today."

Would you have been as proud if I hadn't topped out? I pushed the thought away. But it turned out Dad didn't mean that at all. He spoke slowly, looking out over the lights far down in the valley, groping for the right words.

"It took courage to do what you did tonight. Coming to

find me, not knowing what the consequences would be. As much courage as climbing to the top of that wall, maybe more. The kind of courage I don't have. Courage to run into a burning building—sure. That's different. That's easy."

Dad stopped talking and reached out his arms to me. I buried my face in his MooZical Milk windbreaker, breathed in his Dad-smell . . . and there was nothing more to say.

Dinner was over; Nick would be back from the Igloo any moment. I was sitting in the kitchen on two chairs with my foot up on cushions, my ankle firmly bandaged and a pack of frozen vegetables doing duty as an ice pack. Mum and Dad cleared the table while I told the story of my climbing again from the very beginning, more slowly this time, and complete with all the details. They didn't say much; just tidied and washed and dried and exchanged the occasional smiling glance . . . and listened.

At last, Mum stashed away the final saucepan and scooped up Madeline and her teddy bear. "Tory!" ordered Madeline.

Mum laughed. "You've had two stories already, Miss Muffet," she reminded her, "but you can sit by the fire and play with Teddy while I catch up with my mending. If you can manage to come through, Pippin, I'll settle you on the sofa with your book."

I struggled to my feet to follow them, glad of Dad's strong arm to lean on. We made our way toward the door . . . and that's when I noticed the pile of mandarins in the fruit bowl. They seemed to be calling out to me with little orange voices. *Yes!* If I was ever going to crack it, today was the day!

"Hang on, Dad—there's something I have to do!"

I scooped up a double handful and shuffled on through to the living room, opening the door with my elbow. *"Philip . . ."* Dad was hot on my heels, his warning growl warming me to the tips of my toes.

"Please, Dad! Hey, Mum, Madeline—watch this! I won't drop them . . ."

There was an excited crowing sound from Madeline's corner. She wanted to play the Mandarin Game! But right now, I had other things to do. Juggling with mandarins. Five of them. I knew I could do it. I steadied myself on my good foot, the sore one just touching the carpet for balance. I took a deep breath . . . and focused.

One . . . two . . . three . . . no problem. Spinning in a perfect, even, high cascade. Now or never—if I didn't get the other two up soon, I'd drop the lot!

Four . . . five . . .

And the magic happened. Five mandarins.

A five mandarin cascade—and it was holding. On . . . and on . . . and on . . .

I couldn't believe it—didn't dare take my eyes off them, for fear I'd lose it.

From somewhere far away, I heard the doorbell ring. Nick, back from the Igloo. Out of the corner of my eye, I saw Dad head off to open the door. *"Nick!"* I yelled. "Hey, Nick—come check this out!"

Dad's voice calling: "Pip? *Philip!*"

"Sorry, Dad!" I yelled back. "Just give me a minute, okay? I can't come right now! I've got it! I've truly— *finally*—got it!"

The sound of the front door slamming. Still, I didn't take my eyes away from the pattern of spinning, dancing oranges.

Then Dad was shouldering the door open and standing in the doorway. The bushiest mustache in creation couldn't have hidden his grin. The hugest, shiniest silver cup I'd ever seen was held triumphantly above his head.

"Philip McLeod—you did it! *You won!* Beat the lot of 'em! That old judge came by to drop this off. They overruled the objections; the other boy climbed and fell, less than halfway. You won it, Son—*you won the whole darn thing!*"

And still, I didn't take my eyes off the mandarins. I could see Dad and the cup and the grin beyond them, an unfocused backdrop to the spinning curtain of gold. It was like watching Dad through a veil of flickering, dancing flames.

And then his face changed. He was staring at something with an expression I'd never seen before . . . staring across at the corner of the room.

Mandarins scattered in every direction as I lost concentration and turned to see what he was looking at . . . what Mum was looking at, their faces melting into the strangest mixture of laughter and tears, the proudest faces I'd ever seen.

A tubby little person in shabby pink pajamas was making her slow way across the floor, starfish hands held out toward Dad and me. Step by wobbly step, straight—or almost straight—across the room toward us.

"Well, how about that!" rumbled Dad. "Kid's a McLeod through and through, after all. Show her a silver trophy, and she's off her backside and going for it like she's been walking all her life. That's my girl!"

I gave an inward sigh. Typical Dad. Even if he changed on the outside—about some things, like soccer—he'd never change deep down. Any more than I would. We'd just have to settle for each other the way we were . . . love each other the way we were.

I looked at my little sister making her unsteady way across the room, and smiled. I knew where she was headed—and it wasn't toward the trophy.

Madeline wanted the mandarins.